HEAD OR TALE

SIX EROTIC SHORT STORIES

BY
R. DANIELS

authorHOUSE™

1663 LIBERTY DRIVE, SUITE 200
BLOOMINGTON, INDIANA 47403
(800) 839-8640
WWW.AUTHORHOUSE.COM

First published by AuthorHouse 12/30/05

ISBN: 1-4208-6405-X (sc)
ISBN: 1-4208-6406-8 (dj)

Library of Congress Control Number: 2005905233

Printed in the United States of America
Bloomington, Indiana

This book is printed on acid-free paper.

Cover illustration by Moses Avila

To all the women I have truly loved.
You, who have influenced and inspired within me the
Good, the Bad, the Ugly, and the Horny.
You know who you are.

FROM THE AUTHOR

There are many unexpected occurrences in life, so I felt the need to share the fact that this collection of short stories happens to be one of them. A few years ago, a friend of mine was traveling overseas but did not have sufficient reading material to last the entire trip. I decided to write an original short story with an erotic twist. As a result, the short story entitled *Playing Doctor* came to exist. Upon reading this tale some years later, another friend asked if I would write another erotic short just for her. I complied happily. It wasn't long before several of my friends had read my erotic writings and began to suggest that I compile them into book form. After much coaxing, I finally decided, "Why not?" Here's to all who urged me forward and supported my desire to write and be read. Let's see where this story goes.

CONTENTS

THE INTRUDER

By
R. Daniels

ONE

The room was dark. The air was cool from the soft September breeze that soothed the rigid, towering edifices of the Manhattan skyline. Even though she was fully dressed, covered from head to toe, she could still feel the breeze as it crept through the screen in the open window. A sudden chill shot up her spine. If she were alone in the apartment, she might have moved to slide the window shut. But she wasn't alone. Someone was there with her, and from what she could surmise from the sounds she'd heard thus far, *that* someone was not alone either.

She had been crouched behind the large bed in the bedroom for almost ten minutes now. That's how long it had been since she knew that someone else was in the apartment with her, and now, they had finally made their way to the bedroom. Despite the fact that she held a fully loaded Desert Eagle in her right hand, a gift from her recently deceased father, a spear of fear sliced through her.

She glanced at the window. *Screams? Will anyone hear the screams from the penthouse on the fifty-first floor?* she wondered. It was too late to think about it. The door to the bedroom swung open. She noticed how casually the door was pushed aside, as if this was just an ordinary night for them.

She held her breath as someone walked into the room. She heard a male voice say, "Get the light." They had no idea she was there. But that would change as soon as the light came on. It was now or never. She exhaled sharply, rested her right hand, which held the weapon, firmly in her left, and rose to her feet. She swung the gun in their direction as the light illuminated the spacious bedroom.

Imagine their surprise, she thought to herself. Fortunately, she didn't have to imagine, for the surprise was evident in both of their expressions. They expected to turn on the light and find an unoccupied bedroom. Instead, they found a stranger, clad from head to toe, in black.

She wore a black ski mask, with black make-up covering the skin under the eye and mouth holes to prevent her race from being discerned. The mask was tucked securely into the top of a thin, black turtleneck sweater. Form fitting black pants that caressed the lower half of her shapely frame were held firmly in place by a matching belt. Black shoes, socks, and a pair of thin, black gloves completed the dark ensemble. She surmised that the only two things that exposed her gender were the shape of her figure, which was undeniably feminine, and her smoky voice when she spoke. "Shut up," she said firmly. She pointed the gun at the female who had accompanied the male into the bedroom, and then repeated, "Shut up, shut up. Don't make a fucking sound."

Although her eyes moved in the direction of the male, the gun remained fixed on the woman. "Do as I say and nobody will die tonight." She smiled to herself. She was in control. She took a small step to her rear and reached back with her left hand. She felt for the window and slid it shut. Her eyes never left the male. She breathed in deeply and exhaled ever so slowly. She relaxed her shoulders. She placed her left hand back under her right to support the weight of the gun and took a small step forward.

"Now," she began, "both of you, walk outside into the living room. Move slowly and don't try anything funny. Make no mistake. I *will* shoot you. When you get to the living room, I want you both to sit down in the middle of the floor. Got it? Good. Move!"

TWO

As Ray and Beth sat in terror on the living room floor, the Intruder circled them slowly. Ray, in a pitiful attempt to display valor and indifference, looked straight ahead at the living room wall that stood about fifteen feet in front of him. Beth, on the other hand, kept her eyes glued to the black clad stranger who had taken them prisoner unexpectedly in their own home. Beth had no intention of feigning bravery. She was terrified. Although she made no sounds, a stream of tears ran from each eye, down past her cheeks to her jaws where they collected briefly before dripping off her face onto her dark red sweater. The Intruder, completing what seemed like her one hundredth circle around them, stopped finally about ten feet from where they sat. She said nothing. She simply stared. Finally, after about thirty seconds, Ray spoke. "Listen, you can take whatever you want, okay? Anything you want, just don't hurt us. Please."

"Anything I want, huh?" the Intruder asked. "Well, that's mighty generous of you, Ray, considering the position you're in right now."

Ray's jaw dropped. "How...do you know my... name?"

The Intruder walked over to the bar that sat off to the left and picked up an envelope. She brought it to him and dropped it in front of him. "That is your mail, right?"

He said nothing.

"Of course it is," she continued. "Raymond Del Rio. That's you, is it not?" She shifted her gaze to Beth. "And you. You're Elizabeth Carter." She giggled softly. "Sorry, Beth. No mail for you today."

"Then how do you know who she is?" Ray blurted out, feeling truly bold all of a sudden.

"Oops," she said sarcastically. "You got me. I can't pull anything over on you, can I, Ray Luv?"

Beth turned to Ray. He turned to her. Ray Luv was a nickname that

Beth had given him. It was an affectionate moniker that he repeated proudly to anyone and everyone who would listen whenever he felt the need to display how much of a man Big Ray Del Rio really was.

The Intruder walked over to Ray and pushed the barrel of the gun up against his forehead. "You'd be surprised what I know about you, Ray." She kept the gun against Ray's forehead but turned her attention to Beth. "I bet you'd be surprised what I know about Ray, too."

Underneath all the tears, Beth was confused. The Intruder giggled. "Don't worry, Beth. All will soon be clear. Not only am I going to tell you what I know about Ray Luv here, but I'm going to show you." She looked back at Ray. He was choking back tears of fear. Slowly, the Intruder moved backwards to her original position, all the while keeping the gun trained on Ray. She lowered the gun abruptly and looked at Beth. "Beth, there's a large rope in the corner behind you." Beth looked cautiously behind her and saw the rope, then looked back at the stranger in black. "Go get it and bring it to me. Move slowly, Beth. I wouldn't want to have to shoot Big Ray over here."

"You know so much about us," Ray managed to say over his escalating fear. "Who are you?"

The Intruder smirked. "I'm Batman!"

Beth, being careful not to make any sudden movements, retrieved the thin rope that had obviously been placed there by the Intruder. She turned and began to walk slowly across the room towards her captor.

The Intruder watched Beth as she approached her. She surmised that Beth stood at about five feet, five inches. She had straight, blonde hair that bobbed just above her shoulders. Her eyes were brown, as were her eyebrows, which only proved to the Intruder that blonde Beth was really brown Beth. Something she already knew anyway. All of Beth's features were thin and non-intimidating: her lips, her nose, her chin, all of them save her breasts, which the Intruder noted as almost too large for Beth's thin frame. Beth wore a dark red cardigan sweater, which covered a white T-shirt. She wore a pair of tan khakis that were cinched at the waist by a woven belt that matched the color of her sweater perfectly. She wore no socks inside the open-toed, brown sandals that were on her feet. 'The cool air outside obviously doesn't bother her,' the Intruder thought. She also noticed that Beth wore the same shade of red on her toenails and her fingernails. *She went and got her nails done today. No doubt on 57th street, as usual,* the Intruder guessed.

Beth crossed the distance between the corner of the living room and the darkly dressed stranger. She stopped in front of the Intruder, held out the rope, and said nothing. The Intruder gestured towards Ray. "Tie him up, hands behind him, then roll him over onto his back." Beth began to turn slowly towards Ray. "Oh, and Beth...I know you used to be a girl scout, so you better tie him up nice and tight or I'm gonna shoot his most important parts off. Understood?" Beth tried to hold back another rush of tears. She failed, and nodded. "When you're done, there's another rope on top of the bar. I want you to tie his feet together, too."

Beth set herself to the task of securing Ray's hands behind his back. Once she had him tied up, she rolled him over carefully. Ray cursed at the Intruder as Beth stood and went to the bar to retrieve the second length of rope. Beth knelt at Ray's feet and the Intruder called to her. "Before you tie his feet up, I want you to pull his pants and his underwear down around his ankles."

"What?" Beth questioned. "Why?"

"Just do it," the Intruder ordered.

"You fuckin' twisted-ass bitch," Ray spat at the Intruder. "Fuck you, you crazy bitch. Fuck you!"

"Huh? What?" The Intruder laughed. "Fuck me, huh?"

"Why are you doing this?" Beth asked through a flood of tears. "Isn't it enough that we're helpless right now?"

The Intruder pointed the gun at Beth. "Just do it," she shouted. Beth cowered at the sound of the Intruder's voice and began to cry harder. She fought to stifle her cries and hold back her sobs, but to no avail. She went to work quickly, lowering Ray's pants and underwear, leaving him naked and vulnerable from the waist down. She tied his ankles, making sure the rope was secured tightly.

"Good," the Intruder said. "Now go sit in that chair over there." She gestured to a chair that had been removed from the bar and was now sitting by the fireplace. Beth complied quickly. As soon as she sat down, the Intruder produced a large manila envelope from behind the couch.

"What do you want?" Ray screamed at her.

The Intruder turned and walked over to Ray, who was now sprawled out on the living room floor with his four extremities secured. The Intruder crouched next to Ray and raised the gun in the air. She brought it down hard on his forehead, striking him with the butt of the firearm. Ray screamed in pain and surprise. He looked back at her. The expression on his face told her that he felt the large, bleeding gash that resulted from the blow. His expression also told her that she now had his full attention. She knelt down and whispered softly in his ear. "Shut the fuck up, Ray. You're starting to piss me off. Got it?" Ray remained silent. "Good. I'd hate to have to stick this gun up your ass and blow your *brains* out." The Intruder stood and looked at Ray from head to toe as he lay partially naked in front of her. Her eyes focused on his exposed genitalia. "Aw, Ray. Look at that. All this brutality has caused you to shrivel up on me." She looked back into Ray's eyes. "And here I was thinking that you liked it rough. You do like it rough, don't you?" She shifted her gaze to Beth. "Doesn't he?"

Beth continued to cry.

"Well, this will not do." The Intruder gestured to Ray's limp penis. "Beth, I'm going to need this thing in working order. Why don't you come over here and give Mr. Happy a reason to live."

"What?" Beth sobbed.

The Intruder pointed her gun at Beth. "Don't make me spell it out, Sister. Come over here and go down on your man. I need him hard."

Reluctantly, Beth rose and moved to where Ray lay helplessly bound. The Intruder crossed slowly to the center of the living room and turned as Beth stared at Ray's lifeless member.

"What's the matter?" The Intruder snapped. "You've been handling that machinery for five years. Don't get shy now." She reinforced her words with a shake from her Desert Eagle in Beth's direction.

Beth did her best to choke back tears as she reached for Ray's sagging penis. Her hand wrapped around the base of his unit and the head bobbed to one side. Ray looked at the Intruder, his eyes burning with hatred and fear. The Intruder peered at him from behind her dark mask and smiled. "You got something to say, Ray Luv?" Ray grunted but said nothing. "Good," she said and shifted her gaze to Beth. Beth was trying not to stare at her, but she couldn't help it. Though she was absolutely terrified, she couldn't help but wonder how this stranger could know so many intimate details of their lives, and especially about Ray.

The black-clad stranger waved her gun at Beth, and Beth lowered her head slowly to meet Ray's dangling penis. Normally, his member would've already been rock hard in her hand, but tonight, it was if the penis was as worried about the Intruder as Ray was. Beth opened her mouth and slid the flaccid organ between her lips. She closed her mouth on it and allowed the warmth and wetness of her tongue and cheeks to caress his manhood. Instantly, blood began to pump into his limp unit, engorging and lengthening it with every beat of Ray's heart. Beth began to suck on him in long, even strokes, up and down, allowing her tongue to cradle the underside of his rapidly growing penis the entire time. Ray closed his eyes in spite of himself. He had been around the block quite a few times in his thirty-one years, and had been serviced orally by many different women. Ray knew, like most men, that not every woman knew how to give a good blow-job. It involved so much more than just putting a penis in your mouth; it involved proper suction, the covering of the teeth, tongue placement and the all important amount of inches that went into the mouth during each rise and fall. Some women neglected to lick up and down and around the shaft from time to time, while others were oblivious to the extreme pleasure men derived from having their balls licked. Also, many women lacked the knowledge, let alone the skill, to give a perfect hand job, which was horribly underrated, while they rested their jaws. Some women gripped too tight and pulled at the skin, a most unpleasant shock in the midst of receiving one of life's greatest privileges. Most women had no idea that a skilled hand job (*skilled* being the operative word), could be as equally satisfying as a blowjob. To the chagrin of many men, most women simply took for granted that a man would be happy with *any* grip on his penis, not one that they liked specifically over another. Luckily for Ray, he hadn't experienced any of those problems with Beth in the entire five-year period they were together. When it came to fellatio, Beth was a pro.

Her tongue lashed out at his, now large, throbbing member. She licked at the base of his hard shaft and ran her tongue up and down the length of it. Her hand gripped his wet unit lightly while her tongue pressed against the underside of his balls. Ray tried unsuccessfully to stifle a moan of pleasure. Beth licked around and around his fat testicles. The hand on his penis moved in perfect time with her tongue as it covered every inch of his scrotum. She moved her head lower. Her tongue stabbed at the small area below his testicles. Ray released another sigh of pleasure. Beth pressed her whole mouth against the small area and drove her tongue into his flesh. She inhaled his scent and a sudden stream of wetness gushed between her legs. As her hand began to jerk his member more rapidly, her other hand reached around and grabbed his buttocks. She was becoming so caught up in the act that she almost forgot the Intruder was still there watching every move.

In the center of the living room, the Intruder looked on intently. Underneath her black pants, her own underwear was full of feminine dew. She pressed her legs together slightly and adjusted her weight from one leg to the other. She felt the warmth spreading inside her. Her loins became increasingly hotter as she watched Beth perform flawlessly on Ray's extremities. She wasn't at all surprised at how turned on she had become from watching them. This happened every time she invaded someone's home and carried out her own brand of justice. She couldn't explain why forcing someone else to perform sexual acts in front of her turned her on so much, she just knew that for as long as she could remember, it just did. She ran her tongue across her lips as she watched Beth move back to the tip of Ray's penis and take it hungrily into her mouth. She knew if she watched any longer she was going to explode all over herself. She shook her head and snapped herself out of the sexual trance into which she was falling. She raised her weapon and took a step towards the helpless couple.

"All right," she said. "That's quite enough. He seems to be very much awake now." Beth stopped and looked up at the Intruder. The black-clad stranger retrieved the large envelope she held earlier and tossed it to Beth. "Here, Beth. Now that you've just had that thing in your mouth, take a look at where else it's been lately."

THREE

The envelope landed next to Ray's exposed left thigh.

Beth stared at the large envelope. The Intruder could tell that Beth didn't want to open it for fear of what she would find. Truth be told, Beth had her suspicions about Ray's fidelity already, but she always told herself the one lie that almost every woman tells herself when she knows she can't handle the truth. *'He would never cheat on me, and I know it.'* Denial.

Beth looked at the Intruder. The black-clad female said nothing. She didn't have to. She knew Beth would open the envelope whether she urged her or not. Slowly, Beth reached down and picked it up. She opened the seal and stuck her hand in. Then, she paused. She turned and looked at Ray, who still lay there, helpless and exposed. She saw fear and worry in his eyes but she knew it was no longer a result of being held captive in his own home. No. Now he was worried that Beth would see whatever happened to be inside the envelope. He wanted to say something, but nothing came to mind.

For years, Ray had sweet-talked women. He cajoled and persuaded them into sexual rendezvous, adulterous behavior and lewd acts, all to satisfy his own insecure sense of manhood. Ray was a talker, one who always knew exactly what to say to a woman. If Ray wanted a woman and she showed the least bit of interest, he made it his personal goal to have her, to bed her and give her the types of uninhibited pleasures that some women only dreamed about. When it came to sex, Ray had no boundaries to what he would do. If an act would make a woman feel good, make her come harder than she ever had before, or make her want him even more, he would do it regardless of how kinky or risqué it was. Ray told himself that he was selfless in that way. But now, at the moment when Beth was about to see just how selfless he had been, Ray had nothing to say.

Beth pulled her hand out of the envelope. In her grip was a small stack of glossy, black and white, 8 x 10 photographs. She brought them up to her face as she looked slowly through them one by one. Ray craned his neck in an attempt to see what she was seeing, but Beth held them close. Slowly, her expression changed. The tears of fear changed gradually to tears of anger. Her upper lip quivered as she fought to contain her rage. Ray saw this and his balls began to sweat. Beth was the sweetest woman in the world, but she had a terrible temper, and he was still tied up.

The Intruder stood and watched quietly. She glanced down at Ray. He shot a quick glance back at her. She blew him a silent kiss, taunting him.

She redirected her attention to Beth. Beth had stopped filing through the photos and was staring at Ray. The expression on her face had transformed into shock. Her jaw hung low as tears cascaded down her cheeks.

"What?" Ray questioned innocently.

The Intruder took a step closer and peered at the photo on top of the stack. "Ah," she said to Ray. "Beth has seen photo number nine. I like to number them, you know. Number nine has you in a rather compromising position with Luz Maldonado. That is her name, right, Ray Luv? You know, the girl from the gym on 20th and 6th?"

Beth turned to the Intruder. The Intruder didn't miss the beat. "Oh, Beth," she feigned ignorance, "aren't you a member there? Surely you recognize her." Unfortunately for Beth, she did recognize her, although until the Intruder clarified it, she hadn't known from where.

"Beth, listen to me," Ray began to plead.

"Yes, Beth," the Intruder interjected. "Listen to him. This ought to be good."

"Shut the fuck up, you sick bitch," Ray yelled at the Intruder. His anxiety over being found out had suppressed the fact that he was yelling at a woman holding a very large gun. At the moment, the only thing Ray was concerned about was Beth and her reaction to his indiscretions.

"Sick bitch?" the Intruder asked. She turned to Beth, who was still kneeling next to Ray's exposed lower extremities. "Why don't you check out photo number ten, Beth?" Beth put number nine at the bottom of the pile, uncovering number ten. The Intruder waited while the image in the photo impacted Beth fully before she spoke again. "That's a nice shot, if I do say so myself, wouldn't you agree, Beth?" Beth shot the Intruder a look that said she was not enjoying any of this. "Look at that, Beth," the Intruder continued. "Isn't that the same penis you just had in your mouth? Would you have put it in your mouth had you known it had been parked in Heather Porter's ass?"

"Enough!" Beth exploded. She threw the stack of photos at Ray's face. They slammed against his nose and cut his cheek. She leapt to her feet and kicked Ray in his side. "You fucking bastard, Ray," she screamed at him. "You asshole. How could you?"

"Beth-"

"Shut up," she yelled. "You fucking asshole. How many others, Ray? How many other women have there been?" Ray was truly at a loss. He had yet to see the photos so he had no idea how many different women he had been caught with. "Fuck you, Ray." Beth began to tremble as her anger became too much for her to contain. Beth screamed and fell to her knees next to Ray. She grabbed the collar of his shirt and tugged at it with all her might. "How could you?" she kept repeating through a flood of tears. "How-fucking-could you?"

"I'm sorry, baby. I'm so sorry-"

"Don't you fucking 'sorry baby' me," she screamed and slapped him across the face.

The Intruder stepped over Ray and holstered her weapon. Without uttering a sound, she moved to the door. Her work here was done. Suddenly, Beth sprang from her position on the floor and lunged at the Intruder. The Intruder spun around and caught Beth in her arms.

"Why?" Beth screamed through her confusion and her tears. "Why?"

The Intruder grabbed Beth by the arms and pushed her forcefully to the floor. She stepped forward and glared down into Beth's brown eyes. Though she said nothing, a communication was conveyed between them. Beth looked away and collapsed in a heap of broken dreams and tears on the floor. The Intruder turned, opened the door, and stepped through. She didn't look back.

FOUR

The air became cool as the fresh October night washed over Manhattan. The stars were few but the moon was full and luminous. Beth Carter moved slowly through Tribeca, taking in the distant noises on the busy street just one block over. Over the past five years, she had forgotten how much she enjoyed the natural beat of the city and how young it made her feel. It was amazing how much she noticed about herself now that she was alone.

Beth came to a small alley that was almost hidden between two towering buildings. She peered into the alley and was frightened by the darkness of it. She turned and looked around. There was no one else to be found. She was certain that she was alone. She looked down at the small, brown satchel that hung from her shoulder. As if she were comforting the small bag, she tapped it lightly. Apprehensively, she turned back towards the alley, took a deep breath, and stepped into the dark, narrow walkway.

Her mind raced and she kept asking herself the question, "What the hell am I doing?"

She proceeded halfway down the alley when she heard a slight rustling sound behind her. Her heart jumped into her throat as she spun around in fear. There, in the shadows, she could barely make out the black-clad figure that stood before her. For a moment, Beth neither said anything nor did she move a muscle. Though she had anticipated the Intruder's arrival, she was nonetheless frozen in terror.

As if she had read Beth thoughts, the Intruder spoke. "Don't worry, Beth. You're safer in here with me than you are out there."

Beth choked back her fear and retorted dryly, "I feel better already."

The Intruder took a small step forward, allowing a lost beam of moonlight to lay itself across her black ski mask. "You should," she said.

"You know the truth."

"I suppose I should feel better about that, but I don't."

"You will."

"I'm glad you're so sure about that," Beth said.

"I am. Listen. Don't get all shitty with me. *You* contacted *me*. Remember? I just did the job you hired me to do."

"I asked you to find out if Ray was being unfaithful."

"You also wanted me to present you with evidence that Ray couldn't walk away from."

"So you had me tie him up? You invaded our home and held us at gunpoint."

"I don't tell you how to do *your* job," she said flatly. "Next time, be careful what you wish for."

"I didn't ask you to humiliate me in the process."

"Humiliate you?"

"Yes, goddammit." Beth was slowly becoming infuriated. "You forced me to go down on him *before* you showed me the photos."

"It wouldn't have had the same effect if I hadn't, and you know it."

"What?"

The Intruder took another step towards Beth, bringing her whole body into view. Despite the fact they were now close enough to feel the other's breath, Beth stood her ground. "Don't play dumb with me, Beth. You contacted me because you knew that Ray would talk his way out of whatever accusation you threw at him. You said it yourself when you hired me. You knew that he would lie to you and you'd believe him because you'd want to. You take all his lies, time after time, year after year, and you talk yourself into believing that he's telling the truth, that he would never betray you. Do you know what that makes you, Beth? A fool. For five years you've been humiliating *yourself*, and for what, for whom? A man who'd stick his cock in another woman and then come home and stick that same cock in *you*? No, this is what you wanted. In fact, you wanted evidence that you couldn't walk away from either."

Beth said nothing. She knew the Intruder was right. She also knew that she was not only angry with Ray for his incessant infidelity, but she was mad at herself for not having the strength to walk away. Tears began to well up in her eyes. The Intruder stepped to her side and put her mouth next to Beth's ear. "I'm not trying to break you, Beth. If you want to cry, go ahead, there's nothing wrong with that. But don't cry over the loss of what you had with Ray because it obviously didn't mean enough to him to remain faithful."

Beth wiped her eyes and fought to hold back any more tears that threatened to stream down her cheeks. She turned and her eyes met the Intruder's. Though the Intruder's skin was covered with black make up under her mask, Beth could now see that she had deep, almond-colored eyes. Though her nose was practically rubbing against the fabric of the Intruder's mask, she didn't back away. "The rest of your payment is in the bag," she said, and she thrust the bag into the Intruder's body. Without saying a word, the Intruder took the satchel from her.

Beth wanted to turn and run, but she didn't, she couldn't. Though the masked figure in front of her was terrifying, she was also intriguing. They stood there, transfixed, with their eyes locked. "How do you do what you do?" Beth managed to ask.

The Intruder blinked. She hadn't anticipated the question. "I just do."

"So you've done this before?"

"Why do you ask questions you don't want to hear the answers to?" the Intruder asked.

"I do want to hear the answers," Beth said, keeping her eyes locked onto the Intruder's dark pupils. "I want to know what makes a person grow up and do what you do."

The Intruder stared into Beth's eyes. Her mind kept telling her to 'look away, look away'. But she couldn't. She knew that she frightened Beth, even now when she had no intention of harming her. But the fact that Beth stood her ground and was now staring fearlessly back at her was exciting to her. Deep down, she felt the stirrings of an uncontrollable arousal welling up inside her. What's more, she knew Beth sensed it. In fact, the Intruder was willing to bet that Beth's own inner arousal gave Beth the will and the strength to stand there, staring her down.

The Intruder didn't like that one bit, but by the same token, loved every second of it. Instinctively, she stepped back. Her eyes remained fixed. The last thing she wanted to reveal to Beth was that she, too, like Ray, was just another slave to her own sexual desires. "Like I said, be careful what you wish for," the Intruder said finally. She dropped her eyes and broke the connection. "How long did you leave Ray tied up?"

Beth allowed a smirk to grace her lips. "I looked through the rest of the photos and-" she took a breath to contain the anger that was still circulating through her. "Let's just say I made hell out of the rest of that night for him."

"You left him tied up?"

"I saw him two days later when I went to pick up my things. I still have no idea how he got himself free."

"Amazing, isn't it? The things a person can be driven to do given the proper provocation."

"What I did was different," Beth protested. "I'm nothing like you."

The Intruder stepped slowly back into the shadows of the alley. "No," she said. "But you could be."

"No, I couldn't," Beth snapped. "Not now, not ever." She took a step towards the darkness that swallowed the Intruder. "You hear me, you bitch? Not ever!" Beth stood there in the darkness of the alley. It took her a few minutes to realize that somehow the Intruder had slipped out of the area and was gone. A cool breeze blew into the alley and stroked her face. She looked around. She was alone. It took her another minute to realize that for the first time in a long time, regardless of the darkness of the alley and the recent incidents of her life, she wasn't afraid.

She emerged from the alley into the moonlight and proceeded to the avenue, never knowing that high above her on a nearby rooftop, the Intruder watched her go. In fact, the Intruder watched her until she was so far away that she couldn't see her anymore. Then silently, the Intruder turned and went away as well.

PERSONAL TRAINING

By
R. Daniels

SESSION 1

"Hi. I'm Faith Maxwell. I have a six o'clock appointment with Daria." Those were the first words out of my mouth when the door to the beautiful home in the Hollywood Hills opened in response to my knocking. I admit that I was a little surprised at first. I expected Daria, the personal trainer with whom I had an appointment, to answer the door. Instead, an extremely fit, incredibly handsome black man greeted me. If my description of him leaves anything to the imagination, allow me to put it in terms that you may understand more clearly. He was fucking hot! It's understandable that an initial sighting of this beautifully dark creature would provoke jaw dropping second glances, but I have to explain why this particular circumstance left me feeling a bit uncomfortable. I am a white female, twenty-seven years old, five feet nine and a half inches tall, ten in heels, and I weigh in at two hundred twenty-one pounds. Needless to say, Mr. Milk Chocolate is not who I wanted to run into while dressed in a pair of K-Mart sweats, looking like a fat ol' duffle bag. To his credit, he acted like he didn't notice. He smiled and invited me in.

As we walked through the foyer (yes, the home had a foyer, with a skylight in the ceiling that illuminated the entire entryway), I couldn't help but notice the enormous amount of space. After about twenty feet or so, the foyer expanded into a larger area that branched off into other directions that lead to other rooms and different parts of the house. Off to the right, a large staircase ascended to God knows where. To the left there was a spacious living room with lavishly plush looking furniture, expensive looking art (paintings on the walls and sculptures strategically placed throughout the room), and a huge wood-burning fireplace. Homes like this usually existed only in my dreams or on some cheesy primetime drama to which I'd never admit I was addicted. I half expected Alexis Carrington to jump out and say something derogatorily biting, yet clever and accurate. Alas, no Alexis, just Mr. Milk Chocolate and me, walking down a long hallway that carried the echoes of our footsteps.

As we approached a doorway that I could already see opened up into a very large, well-illuminated room, it occurred to me that I should be paying attention to my handsome escort, as he was saying something to me that I probably needed to know.

"I'm sorry," I apologized. "What did you say?"

He smiled. "I said that Daria's father became ill and she had to leave town unexpectedly this morning."

"Oh?" I said, disappointed. Daria and I had met earlier in the week, where I paid her two hundred bucks for the required, initial four sessions. I also had spent the previous three days filling out some menu form that she had mailed to me so she could help me correct my poor eating habits. Now I'm being told, after all the paperwork prep, not to mention the mental 'psyching up' I had to do to finally tackle my weight problem, on top of the two hundred dollars that I had to dish out before she'd even agree to train me, she's not even here. You don't know how much I hated that skinny bitch at that moment for being beautiful.

We passed through the doorway at the end of the hall. The room beyond opened up into what I can only describe as the biggest home gym I had ever seen (so what if this was actually the first?). This room had everything, or at least everything I would expect a gym to have. There were two treadmills, two elliptical cross trainers, nautilus equipment, stationary bikes, free weights and all these different benches and apparatus that were used for God knows what, dumbbells of all sizes, exercise bands and balls and who knows whatever else? To top it all off, the far wall was glass so I could see the beautiful, king-sized backyard that had a full-sized swimming pool in the far corner. The entire layout was pretty damn impressive. I followed Mr. Milk Chocolate to a desk that was situated at the front of the gym. He picked up a file and opened it.

"Daria left your menu with me," he said. "It's full of meal suggestions and between-meal snacks that should keep your metabolism high once you begin training." He pulled out the menu and handed it to me. "You'll see that the computer calculated the caloric values for each food item and totaled them up for each individual meal. I'm sure you'll be pleased with it."

I didn't even look at the menu. "When do you think Daria will be back?" I asked.

"In about a week or so. You, of course, have the option of waiting for her, or I can step in and begin your training."

"You?" I asked. Despite the fact he was gorgeous, I did not relish the idea of him seeing my out of shape, fat ass sweat while I die on a treadmill. No, thank you.

"Yeah," he said casually, and then laughed. He extended his hand. "I'm sorry, I didn't introduce myself. I'm Aaron, Daria's business partner. We train all of our clients here." I must've appeared doubtful of him because he immediately gestured to the wall in a Vanna White presentation fashion, and pointed out several certificates that hung there. "Like Daria, I hold several fitness and training certifications. I'm fully qualified to train you and get you started while Daria is away."

I had no idea what I was looking at. For all I knew, those were altered copies of his GED. I looked closer at one of the certificates and read his full name. Aaron Thicke. I smiled. "I'm sure you are."

"Then let's get started. Daria briefed me on your goals and needs, and I see no reason why you should put it off any longer. After all, you've taken the first step, you're here and quite frankly, you paid for it." He smiled again. "What do you say?"

I took a deep breath. Even though I paid to be trained by Daria, he did have a point. Why should I put it off any longer? I shouldn't let her absence become another excuse for not doing what I said I was going to do. I'm tired of being overweight, and it was time I did something about it. "Sure. Why not?"

"Great," he said with a big, gorgeous grin. He had all of his teeth, a big plus. "Let's do it."

I put my purse in one of the lockers that sat against the front wall and then followed Aaron out onto the gym floor. We started off with some light cardio, then we moved on to various machines and worked at, what he described as, a heart pumping cardio pace. An hour later, I felt like I was going to collapse. Oddly, though, I felt pretty damn good.

—

That night, my girlfriends and I met at Tequila's for drinks, none of which my menu permitted me to have. So instead, I drank Screwdrivers sans the vodka. Every time I took a sip, I kept hearing that old Tang commercial where the lady says, 'Orange juice. It isn't just for breakfast anymore.' Neither is a shot of vodka and I'd much rather be drinking that. Oh well, Aaron explained to me that eighty percent of my success would come from what I put in my mouth, not what I did in the gym, so I decided to stay committed. Also, sitting in the presence of my three girlfriends, all of whom are much thinner than I *and* are being fucked on a regular basis, was more than enough incentive to be tough and do what I had to do.

So there I was, sitting in a Mexican restaurant on Victory Boulevard with my three closest friends, when inadvertently, I began to take stock.

First, there's Dvorah Garcia. Dvorah is, by far, the best friend I've ever had. We met ten years ago while waiting tables together in New York and have been close ever since. Dvorah is a white, American female of Russian-Hungarian descent who doesn't have an ounce of Latin in her, except of course when her husband, the handsome Javier Garcia, DDS, is giving it to her. Dvorah is 5'6", has brown hair, green eyes and weighs about one hundred thirty pounds. She is beautiful. Her only complaint is that she's slowly developing her mother's wide hips. Please. I'd trade hips with her in a heartbeat.

Then, there's Julia Mateo. Julia is, in fact, a Puerto Rican Latina who just started dating a black guy. Julia stands at a whopping 5'2" and might be one hundred twenty pounds if she's fully dressed and the clothes are wet with bricks in the pockets. She has pecan-colored skin, dark hair and eyes. Men are always trying to get her attention. Her only complaint, for the moment anyway, is that she has a small mouth and it's difficult to orally satisfy her new boyfriend. Life is such a burden.

Lastly, there's Heidi Milner. Heidi is a beautiful African-American girl with dark skin and big brown eyes. Heidi is 5'7" and weighs in at approximately one hundred thirty-eight pounds. She has an ass that would stop traffic and a set of boobs that would give directions. Heidi is an aerobics instructor at Hollywood Hills Fitness, Sports and Racquet Club and has the tightest body I've ever seen. If I were a lesbian, I'd do Heidi. Unfortunately, I'm not into women and Heidi is engaged to a wonderful man whose last name requires seventeen different language degrees in order to pronounce. Her complaint is that her boobs are too big. Compared to the oversized mammary package I'm carrying, Heidi's got the perfect set, and despite what she says, she knows it. No jealousy there, of course.

Then, there's me. Faith Maxwell. I said earlier that I weighed two hundred twenty-one pounds. Well, I lied. It's more like two hundred *thirty*-one. What can I say? I'm a woman, sue me. I have mousy brown hair and bright, blue eyes. I'm told I have a beautiful face. Everyone, from my friends, to men, to my mom, even the mailman, tells me that I have a gorgeous smile. Now, I'm not conceited but I do have a mirror. They're right. As faces go, mine is rather nice. I just wish I wasn't built like a battleship. I'm an auto insurance agent and I spend the majority of my day sitting on my ass at my desk. Not very conducive to losing weight. When I first began talking about hiring a personal trainer, it was Heidi who suggested I check out the trainers at her gym. Then I realized that would entail buying a gym membership and then dishing out additional dough to pay for the trainer. Heidi then remembered that one of the trainers had gone independent about a year or so earlier and was now training privately at her home in the Hollywood Hills. A few phone calls and a referral later, I was meeting Daria on my lunch break and setting up our first session. Daria is an incredibly petite blonde, with a tight body and a warm demeanor. It was her personable manner, along with her physical appearance, that convinced me to sign on the dotted line and hire her on the spot. The girls were surprised when I told them that Aaron Thicke had taken over.

"Thicke?" Dvorah said with a laugh. "Give me a break. Is that his real name?"

"I guess so," I said. "It's Thicke with an 'e' on the end."

"You sure it's not pronounced Thickey?" Julia asked.

"God, I hope not," I answered before taking a swig of OJ.

"So what's he like?" Heidi asked.

"Oh, he's so fine. He's lean and muscular, he's got a cute face, a nice tight butt-"

"Yes," Heidi interrupted. " But is he a good trainer?"

"I guess so," I answered. "He wore me out today."

Dvorah released a devilish laugh. "Yeah, but is he a good trainer?" Leave it to Dvorah to turn any comment into a sexual one. God, I love her.

"We'll find out," I said. "He seems to know what he's doing."

"I'm sure he does," Heidi assured us. "If Daria took him on as a business partner, he must really know his stuff."

"He probably does," I said. "There were all these before and after pictures of their other clients hanging on the walls."

"You sure they didn't grab those pictures off the Internet?" Julia asked.

"No," I laughed. "Daria and or Aaron were in each one, standing by their clients. It was pretty impressive."

"Good for you, Faith," Heidi said as she touched my hand. "I know it's going to work out."

"It will," I said confidently. "I just found it difficult to concentrate sometimes. I mean, this hot guy, while he's helping me out, is leaning over me and touching me to show me proper form and technique. It gets pretty distracting."

"Why don't you go for it?" Julia asked me. "I know I'm pretty happy with my Mr. Milk Chocolate." We all laughed at that.

"I don't know," I said, feeling slightly sorry for myself. "Why would a guy who looks like that want a girl who looks like me?"

"Faith, you're beautiful," Dvorah said to me. She never ceased to amaze me with how much she cared for me. "Stop being so hard on yourself."

"I try not to," I said, trying to sound strong. "But, let's face it, I'm a big girl, and its not just about attracting men, it's about everything."

"Maybe," Heidi said. "But you've got to remind yourself that you're doing something about it, you know? You're not sitting at home just talking about it anymore. That's major, girl."

"That's right," Dvorah chimed in. "And you know we're here to support you every step of the way."

I laughed. "Well I hope you brought good shoes because I want to lose seventy pounds and it isn't going to be easy."

"That's precisely why we're here," Dvorah reminded me.

Julia picked up her Margarita and raised it into the air. "Here's to the journey of seventy pounds. We've got your back."

Heidi raised her glass. "To the journey."

Dvorah picked up her drink and held it up next to the others. "Every step of the way." Dvorah winked at me. "Now pick up that orange juice."

Tears began to fill my eyes. These were my best friends, and they were here to support me. I picked up my glass filled with OJ and raised it into the air. "Aaron Thicke, watch out!"

SESSION 2

Every part of my body was screaming for relief. I think that somewhere between the last set of squats and the second set of lunges, I misplaced my desire to jump this man's bones and was solely concerned with getting through this session alive. After spending twenty minutes of doing something called "Core training", the last thing I wanted to do was torture the lower half of my body. I noticed that Aaron has a habit of saying "We're gonna do this" and then "We're gonna do that," but 'we' aren't the ones doing all the sweating, I am.

He released me from the lunges finally and instructed me to lie down on the mat. Once I managed to get down and lie comfortably, all I wanted to do was fall asleep. Of course, my handsome trainer/slave driver had other ideas. "Now we're going to do some light stretching," he said. *I swear if he says 'we' one more time, 'we' are going to kill him.*

He kneeled at my feet and took hold of my ankles. He told me to relax my legs as he bent my knees and lifted them towards my chest. "We're going to start with a glute stretch." *Again with the 'we' crap.* I would've grabbed him with my thighs and tried to suffocate him if it weren't for that fact that, as he stretched my ass muscles, he began to lean over me to increase the stretch. Suddenly, I found that desire I had misplaced earlier. I caught a whiff of him as he pressed closer. He smelled great, sort of like a fresh Spring-scented lotion. He placed my feet up against his chest (which I could see was strong and masculine under his tank top) and moved his hands from my ankles to the top of my knees. As he pushed my knees further into my chest (as far as my fat would allow, anyway), his triceps bulged and I somehow forgot that I was in pain just minutes before. With my legs raised and bent towards my chest, I realized that if we were both naked, he would be in the perfect position to penetrate me with his, hopefully thick, 'Thicke, Jr.'. He eased up on the pressure and instructed me to relax. I exhaled slowly. "How does that feel?" he asked me.

"Great," I answered and then added jokingly, "Was it good for you?"

"Always," he responded without any visible change in his calm expression. "Breathe in," he instructed me again. I inhaled deeply. He told me to 'breathe out' and he repeated the stretch in perfect rhythm with my exhalation. I flinched slightly as I reached the limit of my range of motion and he stopped pushing. "Are you okay?" he asked.

"Yeah," I answered. "I've never had to lift my legs this far before."

"Well, get used to it," he said. "We're going to be doing a lot of this." My mind went straight to the gutter. "Oh, by the way," he said. "I spoke to Daria. She should be back by the middle of next week."

'No complaints here', I thought to myself. "Is her father okay?" I guess I should at least try to sound concerned.

"She doesn't know yet," he answered. "He's a diabetic. He was admitted to the hospital on Monday."

"Sounds serious," I said.

"It is."

"Is her father overweight?" I asked. I knew that obesity could lead to diabetes. Though I didn't consider myself to be obese, it was always one of my concerns. Aaron read between the lines of my question and smiled warmly.

"No, he isn't," he said as he released my legs and began to extend them slowly. "Don't worry. That's not going to happen to you. You're taking care of yourself now. Okay?"

I looked into his eyes. They were oozing with sincerity. I resisted a sudden urge to take him in my arms and kiss him all over. Instead, I became a little misty-eyed with his show of honest concern. I nodded and smiled. "Okay."

—

"Sounds to me like he was flirting with you," Julia said as we sat in a booth at La Fondue on Ventura Boulevard.

"I don't think so," I protested. I made an attempt to bring my glass of cranberry juice to my mouth but the soreness in my shoulders made it quite an ordeal.

"Oh, come on, Faith," Julia insisted. "The man has your legs bent back with your crotches only inches away from each other and he says 'there's going to be a lot more of this'. Sounds like flirting to me."

"Maybe not," Heidi said. "Stretching is a very important part of any workout. He wants her to be aware of what to expect."

Julia was unwilling to relent. "What do you think, Dvorah?"

Dvorah sipped a glass of red wine. "I think you're having such a great time dating your black guy that you want her to date one, too."

Julia laughed. "Is that so wrong?"

"Not at all," Dvorah answered.

"Where is your guy tonight, Julia?" I asked her.

"He's having dinner with his daughter," she said. "He's going to come by later."

"And what about Javier?" I asked Dvorah. "Don't tell me he's working late again."

"He works late every Wednesday," she explained. "But he always comes home with new porn to watch. He's great."

"That's right," Heidi said. "It's Wild Wednesday."

"They don't call it Hump Day for nothing, baby," Dvorah said with a smile. She eyed Heidi. "And where's Mr. What's-his-last-name?"

"John?" Heidi asked innocently. "He's helping his brother with some 401k thing, setting up an IRA, something to do with money."

"Is that so wrong?" Julia repeated.

"Not at all," Heidi responded. She turned to me and leaned closer. "Enough about me. It's good to hear that you're happy with your trainer."

"I am," I confirmed. "I love the way he seems so concerned with my health and my progress."

"He should be. You paid enough," Julia said.

"No," I responded immediately, feeling like I needed to defend my new trainer. "He really enjoys his work. His concern seems genuine."

"There's one way to find out," Dvorah said.

"How?" I said, knowing Dvorah was probably going to say something off the wall and sexual.

"Give him a blow job," she said casually.

"Excuse me," I said, needing further explanation.

"Give him a good ol' Monica. If he's still concerned after he shoots his load, then he's genuine, but if his concern is all over your sweats, then, hey, at least you've got a good trainer."

"And you'll see just how thick Thicke is," Julia added. "Sounds like a win-win situation to me." We all laughed. The truth was, I really did feel his concern was real, and it only made me want him even more. Just the thought of him made me horny and Friday's session seemed like it was ages away.

SESSION 3

A week ago I didn't know what hip-flexors were. Today, I wanted to rip mine out and toss them into the pool in the backyard. Though I made the conscious decision to hire a trainer, for just one moment of mercy I would have traded him gladly for an hour at Burke Williams Spa and a pack of peanut M&M's. As I pressed back against the weight that sat under my thigh, I glanced over at Aaron, who stood there counting repetitions. I was positive he knew I was close to my physical limit and when he smiled, I expected him to tell me to stop. "Five more," he said.

"Oh, God," I managed to blurt out through my exhaustion.

Aaron leaned closer to me and said, "You can do it." He began counting down my final repetitions, "Four, three, two, one, and relax." I pulled my thigh off the pad and reveled in the temporary relief from the burning in my left hip. I rested my hands against my thighs and bent over to catch my breath. "Awesome, Faith. Good job," he said.

I laughed. "I bet you say that to all the girls."

"I say it to anyone who does a good job," he replied. "I thought I was losing you for a second but you pushed through it. It's worthy of a little praise, don't you think?"

"I guess so," I said. "Lords knows I wouldn't have done it if you weren't here."

Aaron smiled as he led me to the mat to do our post-workout stretches. "Now that I know you have the strength, I will accept no less. I'm going to stay on top of you."

'I wish,' I thought to myself. I smiled at him innocently on the outside, while inside, a line of flames shot straight down between my legs and ignited the pool of sexual gasoline that rested there. "That's why I hired you," I managed to say.

He chuckled. "Actually, you hired Daria. I just happened to take over."

'Just say the word, Baby,' I thought. 'You can take me over anytime.' God, he was so fine. I know it was insane to think this gorgeous man would be the slightest bit interested in me, but right now, I was feeling downright certifiable.

At the end of the session, Aaron walked me to the door and, again, told me I did a good job. I blushed and thanked him. He looked so sexy standing there in his blue and white Nike tank top and his matching blue sweats that I couldn't resist the urge to hug him. As I wrapped my arms around his muscular shoulders and pressed my 44 DD's into his chest, I felt something firm pressing against my leg. 'Oh my God,' I thought. 'He's hard.' Right then, I felt his hard-on vibrate and then heard an unfamiliar chime.

He stepped back and reached into his pocket. He pulled out his cell phone and looked at the LCD screen. He smiled and pressed the button. "What's up?" he asked in place of 'hello'. He paused a moment, then said, "Hold on a minute." He looked at me and politely excused himself, or more accurately, me.

"Okay, Faith, I'll see you on Monday evening. Same time. Great job today." He nodded to me and before I had a chance to muster a reply, he was back on the phone and deep in conversation. Needless to say, I felt dismissed, so I turned and headed for the door. I know he didn't mean to make me feel that way, so I swallowed my need for more of his attention and took my sweaty ass home. A cold shower was definitely on tonight's agenda.

—

That night, I had the worst dream (or, at least, the worst one I can remember) I've had in months. Actually, it started out okay before everything went awry. Of course, it starred Mr. Tall, Dark and Hot.

I was at the house in the Hollywood Hills, standing in the backyard by the pool. It was a bright Sunday morning and the California sun had warmed the water to a comfortable eighty-two degrees. Did I mention I was thin? Well, I am. I'm not talking 160 lbs, which is my actual target weight. I'm talking about 125 lbs, flat stomach, big tits and a round, firm ass. My dream. My rules.

Anyway, I was standing by the pool next to the diving board. Aaron was swimming his last length towards the deep end where I was waiting patiently in my skimpy-as-hell two-piece that I'm sure I bought at Victoria's Secret the night before. My sexy trainer reached the edge of the pool and, with muscles bulging, dripping and shining from the sunlight, pulled himself slowly out of the water. He stood there for a moment, wearing only a black bikini swimsuit (Some things in my dream are obviously out of my control) and then took two small strides and gathered me into his strong arms. He brought me into his space. Like a kitten, I wrapped my arms around his broad, round shoulders. I felt the strength from his firm, muscular chest squeezing against my breasts as he pressed his body against mine. Our lips touched softly. His tongue brushed lightly across mine and I felt an immediate, moist release between my legs. His arms enclosed around my back and I found myself locked helplessly within his gentle, yet manly, embrace. My eyes opened, only to find his beautiful brown peepers staring right back at me. Suddenly, he lifted me up and sat me on the diving board. (You don't know how wonderful it felt to be physically picked up by a man. In reality, any guy who could possibly lift me would be wearing a red cape and have an "S" on his chest). He took a step back and told me to remove my swimsuit. I stood on the diving board, more than eager to comply. (In real life, the thought of getting naked in front of a man is terrifying. In my dreams, it's heaven).

Aaron smiled at me as I tugged at the strings of my bikini top. The thin laces came undone and I let the top fall from my breasts. I placed my hands on my beautiful knockers and squeezed them seductively. I could tell by the large bulge that had begun to push against his swimsuit that Aaron had become aroused. I reached down and forced the bikini bottom to stretch around my shapely hips and thighs. The little garment fell to the diving board and I kicked it towards Aaron. The bikini sailed past his head leaving my feminine scent on the air. He looked at me and smiled the most evil grin. Now, I was hotter and wetter than ever. This is where the dream took a left turn.

Aaron drank me in with his eyes. "Beautiful," he said to me. He turned and faced the pool. "Come on in," he said before diving back into the warm water. I walked to the edge of the diving board, ready to dive into the best sex (the only sex) I've had in years (four, but who's counting?), when the board started to bend. I thought nothing of it at first, but the diving board continued to curve. A lot. "No," I said aloud. "This can't be happening. I'm light. I'm 125 lbs." I looked into the water, and there, at the bottom of the clearest pool were three large numbers that spanned the width of it. Like a digital scale, the numbers began to rapidly increase. I looked at my reflection in the water. I was still thin, but despite my appearance, I began to feel heavy. I looked at the numbers. 180, 195, 210, 225. "No," I screamed. I looked at Aaron who was wading patiently in the water.

"Come on in, baby," he urged me. "The water's warm."

The diving board continued to bend. By this point, the edge of the board was dangerously close to touching the surface of the water. I knew in my soul that the board was going to snap any second. I looked at the numbers again. 300, 400, 500 lbs. Tears began to fill my eyes as I lost my balance and slipped from the diving board. I felt every pound in my body pulling me as I fell into the pool. A tidal wave of water was displaced and shot up everywhere as my *thin, 675 lb frame* broke the surface and dropped like a cannonball. The large cascade of airborne pool water carried the large numbers in the pool, as well as Aaron, away. I felt myself come in contact with the bottom of the pool, and suddenly, I awoke, trying to catch my breath. I found myself safe in my own bed. Safe, alone, and still two hundred thirty-one pounds. *Shit!*

—

"We all have bad dreams from time to time," Heidi said, doing her best to comfort me over the phone.

"I know," I said. "I just feel like I'm never going to be thin."

"You just started," she responded. "Have some faith."

'Have *some* faith', as opposed to the usual 'have a *little* faith'. Heidi knew that, as a teenager, the other kids in school used to make fun of me by saying 'Have a little faith,' then point at me and say, 'Oh, I'm sorry. We can't.' I hated that so much.

"You knew that this was going to take some time," Heidi continued. "This is a journey, remember?"

"You're right," I conceded. "It was a stupid dream." I released a heavy sigh (no pun intended), and concluded our conversation. Heidi was getting ready to go to lunch with her man when I called and, although she didn't say it, I could tell I was holding her up. Dvorah was out shopping with her husband, and Julia didn't answer her cell phone. No doubt she was curled up next to her new boyfriend. So there I was, alone on a Saturday morning.

"I'll call you later," Heidi promised. She would call, too. My friends are the best. "Cheer up, okay?"

"I'm fine," I assured her. We said our goodbyes and I hung up the phone. I sat around for another hour or so before I showered, got dressed and headed out the door. An hour later, I found myself walking through the doors of the Church at Rocky Peak in Chatsworth. Don't ask me why I ended up there. Maybe I still needed someone to talk to. Maybe I needed to talk to someone that, strangely enough, I don't talk to nearly as much as I should.

The church was empty. I walked slowly to the front of the church and stopped at the first pew. There, after much physical demand, I managed to lower myself onto my knees. I put my hands together and closed my eyes. For more than an hour, I prayed. I prayed for strength, I prayed for love, and I prayed for *Faith*.

SESSION 4

Monday after work, I was tired as hell but I forced myself to go to the house in the Hollywood Hills to meet Aaron for my next training session. Traffic was unusually light so I arrived ten minutes earlier than usual. I grabbed my bag with all of my frumpy looking gym clothes stuffed into it and walked the long driveway up to the door. It was open, so I let myself in and headed for the gym at the far end of the hallway.

As I entered the gym, the sound of Aaron's laughter to my far left caught my ear. I smiled and looked in his direction. My smile vanished instantly. Aaron wasn't alone. There was a woman there, probably one of his clients. She was a black woman. Thin. Athletic looking. Great body. She was wearing a tight, form fitting sweat suit that hugged every perfect curve. Her back was to me so I couldn't see her face but I'm sure she was beautiful. Her arms were wrapped around Aaron's neck. She kissed him quickly on the lips and said, "Thank you, baby. I'll call you later." My heart sank. I don't know why I was surprised. Why would a man who looked like Aaron want a woman who looked like me?

The woman turned around. To my surprise, she was considerably older. I'm not talking ancient or anything, but I could tell she was probably in her early to late forties. Still, just as I had guessed, she was beautiful and incredibly well kept. Why wouldn't she be? I'm sure anyone receiving Aaron's professional attention looked great.

The woman walked towards me and flashed a gorgeous smile. Damn her and her perfect teeth. "How are you?" she said politely as she grabbed her purse. I didn't respond. I simply conjured up my best smile and nodded a quick acknowledgement.

"What time will you be home?" she turned and asked Aaron.

"Around 8 or so," he replied.

"Great," the woman said. "Talk to you then."

"Okay," he responded, and then added, "great job today."

"Thanks," she said. She kissed the air in his direction and turned for the door. She smiled at me again and waved goodbye to me with just her fingers. She crossed the threshold and I watched briefly as her perfect ass sauntered away. Aaron's voice caused me to break my stare and turn in his direction.

"Hey, you're early," he said.

Yeah. My timing's just perfect. "Uh, yeah. I punched out early and I beat the afternoon traffic."

"Cool," he said, and then gestured to the restroom across the gym to the right. "Go ahead and get changed. I'm ready when you are."

'Great', I thought to myself. 'Just fucking great.'

My drive and energy level during the session were less than spectacular. While on the leg extension machine, Aaron asked me if I was feeling okay and I lied and told him I was feeling just fine. He inquired about the menu plan Daria designed for me and asked if I was following it. I told him I was (which was the truth) and used the mention of Daria to segue to a subject that didn't require me to answer questions about myself.

"When is Daria coming back?" I asked. The sooner she came back the sooner I could stop training with him. I couldn't believe I allowed myself to have hope. I don't know why I was feeling so bad. I just met the guy last week.

"She'll be back sometime next week," he answered. "She doesn't want to leave her dad until he gets better. He's the only family she has."

"Oh," I said for lack of anything meaningful to say. "I wanted to pay her for the next four sessions." *Another lie.*

"You can pay me," he responded quickly.

"Uh, okay. I left my checkbook at work so I'll bring it on Wednesday." *Three lies in a row.* "Okay?"

"Cool," he said.

"Cool," I repeated. *Shit.*

—

"I wanted to break that skinny little bitch in half," I complained to my girlfriends as I took another bite out of my chocolate cake. To hell with the diet. "I can't wait until Daria comes back."

"I'm sorry, Faith," Julia said.

Dvorah watched as I devoured the cake. She looked at me with the deepest concern. She leaned forward. "Are you sure you want to do that?"

"No," I snapped at her, "but it makes me feel better." Dvorah leaned back in her seat slowly and shifted her gaze out through the Jerry's Deli window. I could tell that my ungracious response to her caring had hurt her. I laid down my fork and swallowed the rich slice of decadence along with my bruised ego. "I'm sorry, Dvorah. I didn't mean to snap at you."

Dvorah's eyes found their way back to me. She smiled weakly and nodded. Though she accepted my apology, I could tell that she was not pleased with my attitude, and I don't mean just my attitude towards her. I could tell she was disappointed with the fact that I was letting my dashed romantic hopes over my trainer, a guy who had no idea that I even liked him (and who obviously already had a girlfriend), get in the way of a goal that is so important to me. She didn't have to say it; I could see it in her eyes. And she was right. I talked such a big game last week when I first started my training, but now, look at me. I'm sitting in Jerry's Deli destroying the biggest piece of triple layer chocolate cake they had in the case. Though I had been following my diet (up until this point, anyway) and showing up for my sessions, I wasn't doing it for me. I was doing it for him. I had lost sight of whom I was trying to make happy in the first place.

I pushed the dish of cake away from me. I looked at my girlfriends. Heidi put her hand on mine and said, "Things are going to be okay, Faith."

I smiled. "I know," I said. "I was stupid to think he'd be interested in someone like me anyway."

The girls tried their best to cheer me up, and for a little while, I did feel somewhat better. Still, once I arrived home, I marched straight for the phone and called Aaron. "I'm afraid I have to cancel our session on Wednesday," I said to him.

"Is everything alright?" he asked. "You seemed a little out of it today."

"I'm fine," I answered. "There's just some work I need to catch up on at the job so I'm going to be tied up late for the next few days."

Aaron didn't sound convinced. "Are you sure? You know, Faith, you're doing so well with your training and your diet. It would be a shame to interrupt your momentum so early in the game. Most people who quit this soon never come back and, consequently, never reach their goal. It's so important that you don't give up."

Goddammit! He sounded so concerned, like he really cared about me. Unfortunately, he didn't care the way I wanted him to so I continued with my defiance. "I'm not giving up, Aaron." I just can't make it on Wednesday, and maybe not Friday either." I paused. Despite the fact that I wasn't going to give in, I still wanted to hear him try to convince me. Telling him 'no' one more time would make me feel like I had power over him in some kind of way, like I was the one in control, like I wasn't the one who would be disappointed.

He was quiet for a moment, and then he said, "Okay." Now, he paused. "Thanks for calling."

"No problem," I said and then pressed the off button without saying goodbye. I tossed the phone on the couch and cradled my head in my hands. I felt like I was back in high school being dumped by Hugo Hamlin again. Hugo was the class nerd/bookworm. He was incredibly intelligent but socially inept. He had very few friends and I was one of the only people who gave Hugo the time of day. Actually, I gave Hugo a little more than the time of day; I gave him the first and best ride of his life. Two days later, he dumped me. It was the first and only time any guy was honest enough to tell me it was because I was fat. His straightforwardness wasn't rooted in malice. It was simply a lack of social graces on his part. After that, I learned to read between the lines. I'm not saying Aaron did any such thing, but seeing him with that woman spared me from approaching him one day only to have to read between the lines once again. Thanks, but no thanks. Getting dumped by the class geek is more than enough trauma for one lifetime.

—

I started dozing off around 10:30 when my phone began to ring. Through half-dreamy eyes, I managed to retrieve the device and press the button. I coughed out an ugly "Hello" only to hear Dvorah's sweet voice come back at me.

She dispensed with the formality of a greeting. "Don't fall on your ass, Faith," she said.

"Well, good evening to you, too," I said to her.

"Did you hear what I said?" she asked me. She knew that I did, she was merely getting me to acknowledge that we were on the same page. This wasn't the first time Dvorah had rang me for a one-on-one, middle of the night, friendship intervention. "You have to hang in there, Faith."

"I will. Once Daria comes back…"

"No," she interrupted. "Now. You've been doing so well lately. And don't tell me it's all because you want to *do* your trainer. This is what you've always wanted. You've had more energy lately and you've been feeling good about yourself. Don't throw in the towel just because you can't fuck the guy."

"I'm not," I insisted.

"Yes, you are," Dvorah countered. "You're down in the dumps because you think some guy doesn't want you because of your weight, when in reality, that's a decision that *you've* made. The guy is living his life, Faith. A life he was already living before you came along. He doesn't even know you have the *hots* for him. How could you possibly know how he'd react if he did know?"

She had a point. I hadn't thought of it that way. I never do. "Should I tell him?" I asked, already knowing what Dvorah would say.

"No," she laughed. "Don't tell him, but don't let this get in the way of your goals either. You want to lose the weight, and until Daria comes back, he's the guy who can help you do it. Okay, so he has a girlfriend. Big deal. That's life, but you've got to go on."

You've got to love the friendship intervention. If you've got a friend who's willing to put up with your shit and still call you to show you they care, don't ever let them go. Dvorah is the best friend I've ever had and she proves it time and time again. "You're right. I know you're right. It's just disappointing, you know? I'm tired of settling for the Hugo Hamlins of the world." I've told Dvorah the Hugo Hamlin story several times over the years. "Every once in a while, I'd like a Denzel Washington or a Brad Pitt or something." I laughed. It was the least I could do to keep from crying. Dvorah laughed with me. Despite our jovial outburst, I was certain she felt my pain. After a moment, I said softly, "I just want to be loved."

"I understand," Dvorah replied. "We all do. It's going to happen for you, Faith. Mr. Right is out there for you. You've got to hang in there until he comes along."

"Hell, Dvorah. I've got to hang in there even if he doesn't."

"That's the spirit," she said.

Once again, true friendship and support had guided me through another bad day. I had made up my mind to go to my Wednesday session. I just hoped Aaron hadn't already filled my spot.

SESSION 5

Okay. So I'm back on the treadmill. I can't say that I'm running or jogging on the damn thing, but I'm walking pretty fucking briskly. Saying that I was already tired after six minutes would be an understatement, but what the hell, I was already tired and the workout had barely begun. Imagine how I would feel if I had actually missed this appointment.

"Hang in there," Aaron ordered me as he increased the speed of the treadmill from 3.5 miles per hour to 5.0. He looked at me to make sure I could and would, indeed, hang in there. I nodded to him as I relinquished the idea that I was going to make it through this workout without having to run. Ten minutes later, I was doing step-ups while doing shoulder presses with 5 lb dumb-bells. I couldn't tell if Aaron was upset at me for canceling earlier, but he was certainly pouring it on today.

"Didn't you tell me once that it was possible to do too much cardio?" I asked in attempt to get him to ease up on the high-energy movement.

"Yes, I did," he responded, visibly pleased that I had retained some of his helpful information. "You want to make sure you stay within your fat-burning zones and not slip into muscle burning. Muscle is what you want to keep. It's what is going to give your body new shape once you reach your goal. And relax."

I took my cue and stepped off the platform for the last time. Those sets were over and I couldn't have been happier. I handed the 5 lb dumb-bells to Aaron and took a large gulp from my Energy-ade drink. "Really?" I questioned him.

"Really what?"

"I'm actually going to have a shape at 160 lbs?"

"Of course," he said and smiled warmly. "Most of the excess fat will be gone and we will have increased your lean body mass. Trust me. You'll be shapely."

That bit of news made me feel good inside. I've always been a big girl so the thought of actually having curves where they are supposed to be seemed impossible. I assumed I'd have to be skinny like one of my girlfriends before I'd see any muscle definition. I shared my thoughts with Aaron.

He chuckled. "Skinny people aren't the only ones with muscle definition," he explained. "In fact, I find that women with a little meat on their bones are much more attractive."

His comment piqued my interest immediately, but I didn't want to seem too eager to find out just *how much* meat we were talking about.

He led me over to the rotary torso machine and I took my place on the mechanism. I was dying to keep the conversation alive so I decided to throw caution to the wind and press the issue. "So the woman I saw you with the other day is close to the weight you like?"

A puzzled look crossed his face. "What woman?"

"The pretty black woman that was all over you when I walked in the other day," I said, trying not to sound jealous. "She kissed you and said she would call you later." I began my first set on the rotary torso machine as he searched his memory for the woman.

He laughed. "Oh. Her. She was not all over me."

"Is that your girlfriend?" I couldn't resist.

"What?"

"Your girlfriend," I repeated. "She was attractive, very petite, older, thin."

"My mother."

I stopped pushing in the middle of my sixth rep and the weight stack slammed back into place. I looked at Aaron for a second in search of any hint that he was pulling my leg. I found none. Still, I laughed.

"No fucking way," I said.

"Yeah, way," he insisted with a nod. "That was my mom. I've been training her for two years."

I felt like such an asshole. "You're serious," I said in hopes that he would let me off the hook and tell me he was joking. No such luck.

"Yeah, I am. She does look great, doesn't she?" he said with pride.

"She used to be forty-five pounds heavier."

"Wow," I said. "Great." Though I was relieved to find out that woman was not his girlfriend but his mom (even better, that's one less pretty woman I have to worry about), I realized we had slipped away from the subject at hand. I wasted no time in steering that conversation back on track. "But that's about the size you like your women to be." Though it came out as a statement, we both knew it was clearly a question.

He leaned in closer as if we weren't the only two people there and someone might hear what he had to say. "Thin isn't *in* with everybody, Faith."

I raised my chin and looked him directly in his eyes. "Strange coming from a personal trainer," I said.

He didn't move. He stayed in close and held my gaze. "Just because I think living healthy is important, doesn't mean I want to fuck a toothpick."

"It doesn't mean you want to fuck a girl the size of a whale, either." There it was. If he previously had any doubts about my own personal interest, they were gone now. I turned my attention back to the physical task at hand. Before I could twist into my first rep, Aaron placed his hand on mine and leaned in again.

"First, I've never met a girl the size of a whale. Second, if you don't want people to think of you that way, you have to stop thinking of yourself that way. Third, I've dated several women your size. In fact, most of the women I date, are."

Inside, my brain was dancing a jig at the Fat Girl Saloon. He couldn't have said anything else that would have been more perfect. Outwardly, my expression remained calm and aloof as if he hadn't just made my day. I considered briefly the fact that he could have said that simply because he knew it was what I wanted to hear, but then I thought, 'Who cares? He said it. Let's roll with it.' I swallowed and forced myself to say calmly, "Well it's nice to know there are still some men out there who judge women for who they are, not what they look like."

He laughed and said, "I'm sure I do that, too, but I like what I like." He pointed at the rotary torso machine and changed the subject. "Hop to it. Give me twenty."

'Baby,' I thought as I became sopping wet between my legs, 'Give me a chance, and I'll give you all sixty-nine.'

—

"You said that to him?" Dvorah asked me later when my girlfriends and I sat in a booth at Café Bizou in Sherman Oaks.

"No," I confessed, "but I wanted to."

"Most of the women I date, are," Julia repeated what Aaron had said to me earlier. "If that's not an invitation to his private gym, I don't know what is."

"She's already in his private gym," Heidi reminded her. "The key word being private."

"I wanted to attack him right then and there," I said.

"He definitely opened the door for it," Dvorah said. "And even if he was talking out of his ass and just said what you wanted to hear, you should call him on it. You never know, you might have a little fun."

"A little fun would be nice. It's been quite some time." I stared at my salad and thought about the one hundred different ways our session could have ended - all sexual. I wondered if I should have pressed the issue further right then and there. Did I miss my window of opportunity? What if he tries to act as if he didn't say it when I see him on Friday? I was happy, terrified and nervous all at the same time. Once again, I turned to my girlfriends for advice. "What should I do?"

They all responded, without hesitation, and in unison. "Fuck him!"

SESSION 6

I had thought about today's session for the last two days. My girlfriends seemed to think that Aaron had opened the door for a more personal relationship, or at least the possibility of one. After all, why would anyone tell you that you're their type if they weren't open to exploration? I mean, he's not married, he's not gay, and he made no mention of having a girlfriend. Of course, it kind of makes me wonder how someone so hot could be walking around as a single man. Oh, God. There's probably something wrong with him. Could he be a control freak? Is he bad in bed? Does he treat his women poorly? Is he all charm but with no real substance? Or worse. Could Aaron Thicke have a small dick? (I mean, I'm not looking for John Holmes here, but, I'll be honest, size does matter). These are questions that had been brewing in my mind ever since I left the gym on Wednesday. Then there's the biggest question. Just because he typically dates big women, does that mean he's willing to date *me*? Maybe he was trying to make me feel better about my size. Let's face it. He *is* a personal trainer. Isn't that his job?

As I panted heavily on the stationary bike, I tried to remain focused on the workout. At times, like the one-minute intervals where Aaron would jack up the level from one to nine, I had no problem keeping my mind on the task. Other times, my imagination was thinking of alternate ways I could be working my body. After fifteen minutes of bike torture, Aaron led me to the incline press to work on my pecs and allowed me to catch my breath. I looked at him to see if he might be stealing quick glances in my direction, but I saw nothing out of the ordinary. Maybe he wasn't interested. Maybe I was reading more into his comment than he actually meant. I decided that I was only torturing myself and made up my mind to turn off my female brain. I found, due to the extra adrenaline from the workout and the excess hormones that were racing through my body as a result, it was quite difficult to stifle the female inquiry that wanted answers, and wanted them now. Yes. It's tough being a girl sometimes.

Mid-way through my second set on the incline press, I developed a cramp in, what Aaron referred to as, my right anterior deltoid. Aaron instructed me to cease the activity and relax for a moment.

"Here," he said, handing me my water bottle, "drink some water."

As I took a swig of H_2O, Aaron circled behind me and began massaging my cramped up shoulder. He pressed his thumb into the knot (ouch) and smoothed it away gradually.

"How's that feel?" he said after a moment.

"Great." I wasn't lying. Having him touch me felt wonderful. The cramp was gone, too. "I don't suppose you'd want to rub my pecs, too." Oh, God. Did I actually say that out loud? I looked up at him and realized I had, indeed, verbalized my thoughts. I must admit that I'm glad that I did. I don't think I'd ever seen a black man blush the way Aaron did at that moment. It was quite an attractive sight.

"Are your pecs sore?" he asked, trying to suppress a grin.

"A little," I said in my smallest, cutest, baby voice.

"That might be inappropriate," he responded. *Cat and mouse, huh? Okay, I'll play.*

"Because you're my trainer?" I asked.

"Yeah," he said. Okay, the cat and mouse game became old to me fast. I decided to cut to the chase.

"Pretend you're not." I don't think I've ever sounded so confident and demanding in my life. I liked it. I think he did, too.

He stood there for a moment and stared into my eyes. My impatience got the better of me and I took hold of his hand (the one that was still massaging my shoulder) and I moved it past my pec muscle to my large DD's. I squeezed his hand and he, in response, began to squeeze and massage my breast. I decided to give him the 'let-me-close-my-eyes-and-release-a-bated-breath-reaction' so he'd know how good it felt. I kept my eyes closed but only for a second. I looked into his eyes. He began to smile. I reached up and pulled at him gently. He circled the machine and knelt by my side. I lifted my head and moved in his direction. Without hesitation, he moved to meet me halfway. Our lips touched. Instantly, I was wet (and it wasn't all sweat).

The kiss started out light. It was obvious that we had to find the bearings that are essential when kissing someone for the first time. It didn't take long. After a few seconds, our lips began to press harder. We turned our heads from one side to the other and we threw our arms around one another. I felt the tip of his tongue graze my top lip. I extended my tongue and pressed it lightly against his. God, I loved kissing him. It was fantastic, not too wet, or too hard, or too wild, but just the right amount of pressure. His mouth fit perfectly against mine. And like me, he didn't make that loud smacking sound that most feel you need to make while kissing. It was quiet. I was in heaven.

We remained locked in this hot and heavy embrace for about five minutes before Aaron mustered up enough restraint to pull away slowly. We stared into each other's eyes and said nothing. I shot a quick glance up at the wall clock. The second hand was just cruising past the three. I looked back at Aaron. Still, we remained quiet. After what seemed like minutes, I looked at the clock again for a quick check. Thirty seconds had passed. Thirty seconds of complete silence. Thirty seconds of visual observation and nonverbal communication. Normally, silence like that would have been unnerving. But this silence was different. It was comfortable and warm. He smiled at me. I smiled back. I would have been perfectly comfortable to sit there all day, not having to say a word. Most women want to hear bells during a first kiss, something inside that tells them this could be someone special. Me? I always wanted to hear this. Communicative silence. I liked it. I needed it. It was something that I had always been looking for, but never really believed existed. And here it was. I couldn't help but wonder if he was feeling the same.

He stood slowly. His eyes remained locked on mine. He reached out and stroked my face gently. "We better get moving," he said softly. "We still have a lot of work to do." He must have seen the millions of questions racing through my mind. How could he not? He was staring into my eyes, the so-called 'windows to my soul'. Believe me, there were no shades or curtains on these windows. At that moment, my soul was completely exposed. He traced his finger across my lips. "We'll talk later." He smiled. Even though I smiled back at him, inside, I was screaming.

Despite the fact that I was dying to jump his bones, I managed to retain my composure and make it through the workout. When it was over, Aaron walked me to the door and kissed me gently on the lips. I fought the girlish urge to say 'call me later' in that 'even-though-I'm-telling-you-to-call-me-later, I'm-actually-asking-you-to-call-me' tone. I don't care how fine he is or how great he kisses, I won't beg any man to call me. So instead I said, "I'll talk to you soon." It was a non-committal way of saying 'if you want to talk to me, call, but I won't be sitting by the phone.' The cat and mouse game is back on, I guess. Question is, who's the cat and who's the mouse? Time to consult the girlfriends.

—

I spoke to each one of my girlfriends over the phone during the course of the weekend. Strangely enough, they each had different advice to offer for reaching the same end: Making Aaron mine.

Heidi advised that I don't call him. "Let him call you. You asked the guy to rub your breasts during a session. If he doesn't have enough sense to make the first call after that, then he's just looking for someone to chase him to make *him* feel good."

Julia's advice was to wait a few days. "You want to let him know that you're interested but you don't want to seem too eager."

"I asked him to rub my tits while he was training me," I reminded her. "That's pretty damn eager."

She laughed. "Maybe so, but you don't want him to think you're some desperate sexual predator who does this type of thing all the time. Trust me, Faith. Wait a day or two. If he calls you in the meantime, even better."

Dvorah's advice was slightly different. "Fuck it, girl. If you want to call him, call him. This is the 21st century. You've already kissed him and he's rubbed your breasts. Why play the game? If you want him, go get him."

I didn't know whose advice to follow. Each of them made sense, and like I said before, each of them was having sex on a regular basis. Their methods had obviously been met with success. The question was, which of those methods was going to work for me. I didn't have to wait long for an answer. Five seconds after I hung up with Dvorah, Aaron called.

"How are you?" he asked in a formal tone.

"I'm good," I returned, equally formal. "And you?"

"Good. Um," he paused. *Here it comes.* "Listen. Daria came back this morning. Her dad is going to be okay, and, um, I think it might be a good idea if you continue your training with her."

"Uh, okay," I said, trying not to sound disappointed.

"I've already informed her of your progress and how hard you've been working, and, uh, you know, she's ready to take over."

"Okay," I repeated, doing my best to sound completely indifferent. "Sure."

There was a silence on the phone. An uncomfortable one. I didn't like it. Finally, he spoke. "So what are you doing tonight?" he asked. His tone seemed lighter, less formal.

"What?" I asked. I heard his question. I just wanted to hear him ask me again. I'm a woman, sue me.

"How about dinner and a movie?" he asked.

My initial inclination was to act like I had to think about it, as if I had something or some*one* else to do. But then I heard Dvorah's voice in my head saying 'Why play the game? If you want him, go get him.'

"Pick me up at seven," I said. God, I sounded confident. Hell, I felt pretty damn confident, too.

I rattled off my Sherman Oaks address quickly and hung up the phone. Before I could do anything else, I called each of my girlfriends to give them the news. After a quick congratulations and another round of advice, I hung up and squeezed myself into a pair of control top panty hose, a comfortable pair of black slacks and my favorite white blouse. I touched up my hair and make up and waited for Aaron to arrive. My buzzer rang at precisely 7:00.

SESSION 7

Dinner was wonderful. We feasted on grilled salmon followed by a light spinach salad at Maggiano's in Canoga Park. Not exactly the signature meal to be eaten at such an authentic Italian restaurant, but, hey, I'm watching my diet and, of course, Aaron was considerate of that.

Afterwards we went to the AMC Promenade Theatre and watched some new Tom Cruise flick. Tom looked sexy, as usual. The leading lady was thin and beautiful, of course. Although the movie was quite enjoyable, it was hard to lend my full attention to it because of the anticipation of what was going to happen once Aaron and I didn't have dinner and Tom Cruise to distract us. I was dying to kiss him again but I didn't want to climb all over the guy while Tom was killing bad guys (or were they police officers?) on the screen.

We arrived back at my one bedroom apartment on Moorpark shortly after 11:30. I took Aaron by the hand and led him to the couch in the living room. It was strange. I was so accustomed to him leading me around the gym that I never imagined I'd be leading him around my home. We sat on the sofa and, once again, engaged in the best make-out session ever. I'm talking even better than the one in the gym. Here, there were no clumsy machines or heavy weights in the way. It was just Aaron and me. One on one.

It wasn't long before we were groping each other under our clothes. His warm tongue stroked my neck and sent a wave of wetness between my legs. I unbuttoned my blouse as to allow him more access to the 'girls'. He lowered his head and kissed a path from my neck to the middle of my cleavage, the whole time licking and nibbling gently on my flesh. I moved my hand down his side and continued to feel past his tight ass. I brought my hand up around his thigh and decided it was time to go in for a quick feel. Time to see what he was working with.

As I made my way towards his crotch, he stopped kissing the tops of my breasts and looked into my eyes.

"Wait," he said.

'Wait?' I repeated the question in my head. I'm about to feel a guy's dick for the first time and he says wait? If I hadn't felt self-conscious before, I most certainly felt that way now.

"What's wrong?" I asked.

He smiled. "Wrong? Oh, nothing's wrong. I just," he paused.

"What?"

"I didn't want to start things off this way. I wanted us to develop a friendship before we jumped into something hot and heavy." I interpreted hot and heavy as sex.

"Oh," I managed to say. How sweet. This hot man has me all dripping and drooling on the brink of my first sexual experience with someone other than myself in four years, and he picks this moment to tell me he wants to be friends first.

"I guess I should've said something sooner," he said.

I laughed lightly. "That would have been nice," I said. At least he didn't wait until I was naked. That would have really fucked with my ego. "Okay," I agreed finally. "Friends first?"

"Is that okay?" he asked.

"Sure. Okay," I answered as I moved my hand quickly around his thigh and took hold of the large (oh, yeah) bulge in his slacks. "Let's start tomorrow."

A look of surprise leapt across Aaron's face. Before he had a chance to respond I was, once again, leading him through my apartment. This time, we went straight to the bedroom.

—

How long had it been since a man touched me in this way? Four years. Four long years. I guess I hadn't even realized how much I actually needed to feel the touch of another, at least not until now. And hot damn. I had forgotten just how good naked skin could feel.

Aaron sat on the edge of my large bed. I had dimmed the lights because, despite the fact I was ready to do this, I was still quite uneasy about being naked in front of such a well-chiseled creature. He moved to my side and kissed the side of my face gently. He sensed my sudden apprehension and whispered, "Relax. You are so beautiful. I knew that I wanted you from the first moment I saw you."

'Wow,' I thought. 'No one has ever said that to me before. I never imagined anyone would. Who am I kidding? Of course I've imagined it, but I never thought it would actually happen.' Still, I released a girlish giggle and used a little levity to mask the nervous anxiety I felt. "Liar," I said. "Say it again."

He began kissing a path down to my breasts, leaving a warm trail of wetness in his tongue's wake. "You're beautiful," he managed to say between kisses. "And I wanted you from day one." His mouth reached the waiting nipple of my right breast. His hot tongue circled the colored flesh before his mouth seized and covered the entire nipple, sucking me in gently. I moaned and held his head against my breast. His strong, dark arms wrapped around my hefty frame and squeezed me. I melted. It felt so good to have a pair of arms holding me, making me feel safe and secure, as if my size didn't matter.

I felt Aaron pressing against me. It was a moment before I realized he was attempting to push me onto my back. I released his head from my bosom (I love that word) and obeyed his unspoken command. As I lay there, Aaron looked up at me and said, "Now. Just relax." *Trust me, baby. I'm going to give it my best shot.*

Aaron nestled himself once again against my breasts and continued to lick and suck each one. His hands (at times it seemed as if he had eight of them) were moving constantly across my body, caressing and squeezing me all over. It wasn't long before Aaron began making another trail towards my lower regions.

'Oh, God,' I thought, 'Is he really going to do it? Is he really going to go down on me?' I was already so hot and horny from him kissing my breasts, I was worried that if he touched my pussy with his tongue, I might come right then and there.

I felt his hot breath on my clit. I tensed slightly. The anticipation of his tongue sliding in and out of me was driving me crazy. I tried to relax, but it was difficult due to every hormone in my body screaming, 'Hurry up and get there.' As if Aaron had heard my silent plea, he moved his tongue lightly across my clitoris. It had been four years since I'd had sex, but it was much longer since anyone had licked me down there. Words cannot describe the feeling. Though I didn't come at that moment, I knew my first orgasm was lurking closely around the corner.

The softness, the wetness, and warmth of his tongue on my clit sent a shock wave through my body. He extended his tongue and licked my pussy slowly from bottom to top. I moaned softly in response to his gentle licking. Aaron repeated it, again and again, thoroughly enjoying the fact that he could obviously provide me with so much pleasure.

He inserted his tongue deep into my pussy. I jerked suddenly and Aaron placed his hands under me at the small of my back and held me firmly in place. *That* felt good. I gyrated in perfect rhythm with his tongue as he probed deep inside of my wetness. My hands, outstretched at my sides, gripped the sheets that covered the bed. With each stroke of his tongue, I involuntarily tugged at the bed coverings.

Aaron pushed his long tongue deeper inside of me and began to increase the speed at which he licked. My body responded to his face rubbing against my pubic bone, his tongue inside of me, and his hands holding me firmly. He began to move the entire length of his tongue in and out of my pussy. My pussy lips throbbed as I felt my climax starting to build. His tongue maintained a steady pace as it darted in and out of my hot, dripping cunt (That's right. I said cunt. I talk so dirty when I'm doing it).

I began breathing heavier and more erratic with each passing moment. As my orgasm drew closer, I began to moan aloud. (Since it was our first time doing the deed, I resisted the incredibly strong urge to yell, "Goddammit, you sexy Black motherfucker. Eat me.") Then it began. I felt the tightness build in my loins. The more he licked, the tighter the feeling became. It felt as if there was a rope attached deep inside of me, and someone was twisting it, causing it to constrict upon itself. The feeling of tightness grew. I began to moan louder, "Oh, God, don't stop. Please don't stop." My body began to jerk uncontrollably as my climax took control of my senses (Yes, I've read way too many romance novels). Aaron continued to lick at me, tasting my very essence. My body shook as the rope deep inside of me finally snapped, sending waves of warmth in all directions throughout my body. The warmth traveled slowly and evenly into my breasts, my legs, my back, and returned into the wetness between my legs. Aaron began to lick me lightly as my body tightened, then relaxed suddenly and went limp on the bed. I tried to regain control of my breathing to no avail. I couldn't believe I'd forgotten how incredible it felt to have someone other than myself touch me in such a way.

As I took a few seconds to regain a little composure (like I wasn't going to lose it again as soon as he touched me), I listened as Aaron took this time to adorn himself with a condom. I don't know where it came from, but kudos to him for having one. A few seconds later, Aaron rose up and mounted me as I lay on the bed. He stared into my eyes as he positioned himself over my body. Right about now, it occurred to me that I hadn't actually seen his cock yet. It felt big through his slacks, but it could've just been bunched up or something. Then, I felt his penis pushing against my pussy lips. I spread my legs farther to let him in. Now I was going to see if Aaron Thicke was truly thick. He pushed himself into me. Oh, yeah. (I repeat! Oh, yeah).

He continued to push his cock inside of me. It felt incredible. It was like having a nagging itch that was being satisfactorily scratched inch by inch as he moved farther into me.

As he began to slide deeper into my pussy, I reached up and pulled him to me. I kissed him feverishly, tasting my own juices all over his face.

Aaron moved slowly at first. Then, as I caught the rhythm and moved with him, he gradually increased the pace of his deep thrusting.

Tiny aftershocks surged through my body as new tremors of sensation raced through me. I raised my legs to allow deeper penetration, and I placed my hands on his broad shoulders as to get more leverage for the counter thrusts. Aaron plunged his cock into me with long, even strokes that filled me over and over again. At this rate, I knew that it wouldn't be long before I reached another climax. I could feel it starting to build already. Thrust after thrust, stroke after stroke, brought me closer to another orgasm. After another ten minutes of his cock repeatedly slamming into me, the tightening inside of me began again. "Oh, yes. Yes. I'm coming again, oh..." I could barely speak as another orgasm shook me from the inside out. Aaron continued to plunge into me as I came all over his long, black dick.

Aaron made love to me for the next hour before he rolled off of me and began pulling me on top of him. I froze. Being under him was one thing, but I'm a big girl. The last thing I wanted to do was hurt this man.

"What's wrong?" he asked.

I was embarrassed by what I was feeling, but I couldn't exactly tell him I had a pie in the oven. "I'm afraid I'm going to hurt you."

"You won't hurt me, baby," he said confidently. "I've been waiting all night to feel you on top of me."

God, I loved it when he spoke to me like that. "Are you sure?"

"Positive. Don't hold back, Baby. Get over here and ride me good."

His commanding tone turned me on all over again (as if I was ever turned off). I slid onto his hard, black cock and I rode him with everything I had. It turns out those hip flexor exercises came in handy. Within ten minutes, Aaron reached his limit. I felt his cock jumping inside of me as he came.

I pulled myself off of him and collapsed at his side. I don't know if I fell asleep first, but I do know that I woke up around three in the morning, horny as hell. I removed the condom that was still wrapped around Aaron and I went to the bathroom to grab a washcloth. I crept back into the bedroom. He was still asleep. Good. I cleaned his genitals gently and then proceeded to suck that black cock back to life. I once heard the best way to awaken a man is to suck his dick. He'll never complain, and believe me, when Aaron awoke, his didn't seem upset at all. After another round of lovemaking, we fell into each other's arms once again.

"How is Daria as a trainer?" I asked as I cuddled up under his arm.

"She's great," he said and then chuckled. "But if you start sleeping with her, too, we're going to have a problem."

"Don't worry." I laughed. "One trainer at a time." Wow. If I'd known exercising would be so rewarding, I would have hired a personal trainer years ago. I'm now convinced that every girl should have one in her home.

Irony. A week ago my size was undermining my self-worth and my self-confidence. Who would've thought my weight would turn out to be an asset? Hot damn! Wait until my girlfriends here about this!

M I L F

By
R. Daniels

1

It was the strangest, most unexpected thing I had ever hoped would happen. And boy, oh boy, did it make my dick hard. I mean, there she was standing in front of me. Naked. Well, except for the white robe. But underneath, she didn't have on anything. I'm talking nothing but a smile.

My first instinct was to look away. Not because I didn't want to see her body. I mean, come on, I'd always thought she was beautiful. Every one who saw her thought so as well. I tried to look away out of respect. But then the little voice inside my head, which was now being amplified by the raging hard-on between my legs, started yelling, "Oh shit. She's naked. What the fuck do you mean 'look away'? Face front, muthafucka." What could I do? After all, she stopped in the doorway and made sure I was watching before she loosened the belt on her bathrobe and let it fall open. Then she spoke. Her words were soft. So soft, in fact, that it took a fraction of a moment before they actually penetrated my brain and sank into my awareness.

"I'm going to go lie down," she said. "I'll leave the door open." She turned slowly and disappeared out of the doorway. I froze. The head on my shoulders was saying, "Don't move", but the head between my legs was imploring, "Move, Goddammit, move". I heard her bare feet climbing the stairs before the amplified little voice said "fuck it" and I began following her to what I hoped was her bedroom. I mean, she may be my best friend's mom, but what's a hot and horny young brotha supposed to do?

As I moved up the stairs, I pinched myself as hard as I possibly could. I needed to know that this shit was real. The last thing I wanted to do was wake up in my bed with my dick in my hand. Nope. No dream. I'm still here in Jay's house, climbing the stairs, following his naked mom. I found the bathrobe lying on the floor at the top of the stairs. My "Johnson" got a little harder. I paused there and stared at it for a moment. I looked in the direction of her bedroom and swallowed. I looked in the other direction towards Jay's room. Normally when I came here, that's the direction in which I would go. His door was closed. I knew he wasn't in there but the closed door made me feel better anyway. I looked towards his mom's room again. Her door was open, just like she said it would be. I tiptoed quietly across the distance between the stairs and her doorway. Why was I tiptoeing when no one else was home? Hell if I know, but that made me feel better, too.

I stopped at the open doorway and peered in. There, lying on her side facing me, was Mrs. Murphy. Damn, she was beautiful. She had light, brown eyes with short brown hair that was cropped tightly against her long, beautiful neck. Through years of jogging and exercise, she had carved out a toned, athletic body any woman would kill for. She had a flat stomach, a round ass and legs like a stallion. Every guy in the neighborhood, teenager and married man alike, had jacked off in honor of this woman at least a thousand times. She was definitely the neighborhood's hottest MILF. For those of you who haven't seen the movie "American Pie," that stands for *"Mom I'd Like to Fuck."* And Lo and behold, I was about to fuck her. She smiled at me but said nothing. She simply fluffed up the pillow next to her and stretched out on her back, the whole time watching me. I thought of Jay. What would he think? What would he do if he was in my shoes and this was my mom? I pushed that gross thought out of my brain. I couldn't worry about that now. I was at the moment of truth and I would've been lying if I said I wasn't going for it. I smiled back at her, took a deep breath, and crossed the threshold.

2

Let me back up a minute and replay the events that led to me to this point. I need to make sure I didn't miss anything or misinterpret the signals being sent my way. Though it's pretty hard to misconstrue this one, I needed to understand how my arrival at Jay's house turned into my greatest fantasy coming true.

I guess it all started early that morning. I came home from a hike up Runyon Canyon and I entered through the front door. This entrance opened up into the living room. Normally, I would've used the side door that opened to the kitchen, but today I was extra tired and the front door gave me quicker access to the stairs that led to my room. As I touched the bottom stair, I heard what I thought was a sniffle. Not the kind of sniffle you hear when one has a cold or sinus problems, this was clearly a 'crying' type of sniffle. I turned and headed for the kitchen, and there, sitting at the dinner table was my mom and Mrs. Murphy.

They seemed kind of surprised to see me. Maybe they didn't hear me come in. I was equally surprised, but for two completely different reasons. First, I didn't expect to see Mrs. Murphy at my house though she only lived three blocks away. Her son, who is my best friend, Jay, had just left for a month-long trip with his dad. Mr. and Mrs. Murphy had been divorced for almost eleven years. The thing was, my mom and Mrs. Murphy had some type of falling out about two months ago. Apparently my mom unintentionally said something pretty fucked up about how 'youthful' Mrs. Murphy dresses. Mrs. Murphy was more than a little offended. My mom dresses like a nun whose middle name is Chastity, which is fine by me. Mom is an attractive woman for her age, but she's nowhere near being the "MILF" that Mrs. Murphy is. Though I didn't hear exactly what sparked the argument, they traded personal insults for quite some time before one of them called the other a 'slut'. That did it. I thought they were going to come to blows, which actually, would have been kind of cool in a 'catfight' kind of way. Mrs. Murphy stormed out of the yard and didn't look back. I asked Jay if he knew what the deal was, but he said his mom was being as tight-lipped about it as mine. I didn't think they would ever make up, until now.

The second reason I was surprised was that both of them were crying, or had just finished crying. I stepped into the kitchen.

"Everything okay?" I asked. I wanted to make sure they weren't going to start scrapping right there on the linoleum.

"Everything is fine, Dee," my mom reassured me.

I turned and looked at Jay's mom. "How are you, Mrs. Murphy?" I hadn't seen her since Jay took off with his dad a week ago.

"I'm fine, Mr. Brown," she said playfully. "I heard it was your birthday the other day."

I smiled and nodded.

"Happy belated Birthday. How does it feel to be eighteen?" she asked.

"Like it did to be seventeen, I guess."

"How was the hike?" Mom asked.

"Good. I feel good. Gotta stay in shape, you know?" I turned to walk out of the kitchen but then I stopped. I remembered that Jay said I could hold on to all his football gear while he was away. "Mrs. Murphy, did Jay leave me a box of stuff before he left?"

"Stuff?"

"Yeah, you know. Football helmet, shoulder pads, stuff like that."

She sniffled then laughed. "I was wondering what that box was sitting in the middle of his room?"

"Cool. Can I come and get it?" Little did I know.

"After you take a shower," my mom said. "You stink."

Mrs. Murphy rose from her chair. "I'm gonna get going, too, Millie," she said to my mom. "I've got some things to do." She turned to me. "Come by in about an hour for the box."

"Okay." I turned as my mom and Mrs. Murphy embraced. I heard my mom say, "I'm so sorry," to which Mrs. Murphy responded, "Me, too." I figured all was 'good in the hood' so I went upstairs, stripped off my clothes and hopped into the shower.

After about forty-five minutes or so I was dressed and ready to go. My mom decided she was going shopping at the mall. She asked if I wanted to come. "Shopping with you is like an all day affair," I said. "No, thanks."

I threw on my sneakers and headed for the door. Mom offered to drop me off at the Murphy's so I took her up on the ride. "You're sure you don't want to come?" she asked as we pulled up in front of the house.

"No thanks, Mom".

"Okay," she said. She seemed a little disappointed.

I jumped out of the car and strolled up the walkway to the Murphy's front door.

My mom pulled away as I rang the doorbell. I waited a few moments and then pressed the buzzer again. Finally, the door opened. Mrs. Murphy didn't step into the doorway but her voice came from around the corner and said, "Come on in, Dee."

I stepped through the doorway and the door closed behind me. I turned and took in the most breathtaking sight I'd ever seen. Mrs. Murphy was standing there in a white terrycloth bathrobe. Her hair was wet and she smelled like Neutrogena Rainbath. Her legs were long, lean and muscular. No doubt the result of all that jogging she does. Just seeing her like that made me harder than a missile.

She pointed towards the living room but headed in the other direction. "Go have a seat. I'll be right back."

I complied and went into the living room. I was a happy guy. I had a raging hard-on and was about to receive some really cool football gear. What more could an eighteen year old brotha ask for? The answer appeared in the doorway with her robe hanging open.

3

So there I was. I was standing next to a bed I never thought I would see, much less climb into naked. I was rock hard and nervous as hell. Sure, I had been with a few girls from the neighborhood, I even managed to bed two from my job at the grocery store, but this was different. She was different. She was no schoolgirl who was learning the ropes like I was. She was a woman.

She looked up at me and smiled. If she guessed I was waiting for some type of instruction, she was right. Don't get me wrong. I knew how to go for mine, but this was one sexual encounter I didn't want to fuck up.

"You gonna stand there all day?" she asked. I shook my head nervously and climbed on to the bed. I remembered I was still wearing my sneakers. I stopped suddenly and struggled to kick them off while trying not to look like a fumbling idiot. I managed to release my feet and continued my crawl towards the hot, awaiting body that lay there. I stretched out next to her and visually took in her body from head to toe. God, she was beautiful. She moved her hand up to my face and caressed my cheek. She smiled and pulled my face down to hers. Our lips met and I swear I almost blew my load right there. I couldn't believe this was happening.

After a few moments of kissing those beautiful lips, she raised her chin and guided my head to her neck. I began kissing her slowly from one side of her neck to the other. I kissed my way up to the spot behind her ear when she released a small moan of pleasure. I didn't think my "Johnson" could get any harder than it was, but I was wrong. She pulled my head closer and I began to suck lightly on her tender flesh. She moaned again and ran her left hand down the front of my body. She stopped at my crotch and cupped at the throbbing monster inside. I moved my mouth around her neck and found the same spot on the opposite side. She moaned again and began tugging at my sweats. The sweats came down easily and so did my underwear. Mrs. Murphy knew what she was doing. She ran her hand up my thigh, grazed my balls and grabbed my shaft. She must have been pleased because she released a pleasurable sounding "Oh!" She raised her leg and placed her foot in the crotch of the sweats that were now wrapped around my ankles. With one strong thrust, she pushed my sweats and my underwear from my body before she began tugging at my T-shirt. I lifted my body so she could pull it over my head. She tossed the T-shirt aside and rolled over on to her back. Then, she reached up and pulled me to her, wrapping her legs around my back. She began to run her hands up and down my body. She grabbed at my ass and pulled my dick into her pubic bone. God, it felt good.

I continued to kiss her neck. Slowly, I began making my way down to her lovely breasts. I licked around the nipple as she gyrated into me. I took the right nipple into my mouth and I caressed the left breast with my free hand. She pulled my weight onto her toned body and grinded her pubic bone into me once more. I maneuvered myself over to her other breast and did my best to give it equal service. She exhaled heavily and released another sigh of pleasure. Her left hand slipped into the space between our gyrating thighs and grabbed my pulsating dick once more. She began to stroke it in rhythm with our movements. I didn't want to come just yet so I moved my tongue down to her navel, causing her to release me. I licked at her bellybutton and came to the realization that there was only one place I could go from there. I had never gone down on a woman before but, hell, what was I supposed to do? Ask for a time out? Yeah, that would've gone over really well. So instead, I trudged on.

As I moved my mouth over her pubic bone, I caught her actual scent for the first time. I inhaled deeply. Her odor was light and pleasantly musk. I slid both hands under her tight ass and pulled her body to me. Finally, I was there. Lightly and ever so gently, I tongued the top of her clit. Her body had a mild spasm in response. I extended my tongue and ran the full length of it up and down her protruding pleasure center.

She released a moan that was louder than any sound I ever imagined she could utter. It was heavy, raspy, and oh-so hot. I continued to lick her lower until I reached the beautiful pussy lips that seemed to be begging for me to kiss them. I placed my open mouth firmly on those two little flaps and sucked them in. I licked feverishly at the lips and parted them with my tongue. Her body jerked and she let out another long, deep moan. Her voice vibrated in time with each spasm that her body generated. She placed a hand on my head and pulled me into her. I grabbed at her ass and beckoned her even closer. My tongue darted in every direction while maintaining a constant, perfect rhythm with her gyrating body. She lifted her legs higher which allowed me to lick even deeper. She moaned again and placed her feet on my ass. I wrapped my hands around the top of her thighs and slid my tongue back up to her throbbing clitoris. Her body jerked as she said, "Oh yeah." Her hands cupped the back of my head and locked me in. She began to gyrate harder and faster against my working mouth. My tongue was growing tired but there was no way I was going to give up now. She tried to say something. At first, it came out as gibberish but then it became crystal clear. "Oh yeah. That's it. Right there. Oh...oh...fuck...here I come... here I...here I..." Her voice trailed off into a long continuous moan. Her entire body shuddered violently against my face as she reached an orgasm that I can only guess felt as good as hell. She stopped moving suddenly and her body stiffened. Her hand held my head in place and her thighs closed in around my ears. I was locked in tight. Houdini couldn't have gotten out of this one. Little tremors must have been going through her body because she began to shake rapidly. Then, all at once, she released a loud sigh and her body completely relaxed under me. "Oh, fuck yeah," she managed to say. I tried to continue licking but she was having no part of that. She pushed me away. "Easy, Tiger," she said breathlessly and smiled.

I sat up and began to wipe my mouth. Like a wildcat, she leapt across the bed and pushed me onto my back. She kissed and licked my mouth clean and held my hands down above my head. I surrendered to her completely as she licked my neck and began moving down to my chest. 'Oh shit,' I thought. 'Mrs. Murphy is going to give me a blow job.'

She licked hungrily at each of my nipples before sliding down to my stomach. She sucked my flesh and moved her open mouth down to the base of my throbbing black cock and then down to my nuts. At that moment, a thought occurred to me. 'Good thing I had just taken a shower. You never know when someone might be licking your balls.'

She ran her tongue over my nuts and began to lick at them lightly. I never thought anything could feel so good. She grabbed the base of my cock with her right hand and ran her tongue up the back of it. She licked up to the head and took me into her mouth. Without even realizing it, I moaned and spoke out loud. "Oh, Mrs. Murphy." With my dick still in her mouth she uttered, "Uh-uh." She took my cock out of her mouth and began pumping it with her hand. "I think you can call me Shannon for now."

I smiled and released a sigh. "Shannon. Okay."

She replaced her hand with her hot mouth once again and resumed sucking on my rod. Up and down in long, even strokes. I was in ecstasy. She continued to alternate between sucking me off and licking my balls ever so lightly. I found myself silently asking the question, 'what was Mr. Murphy thinking when he left this woman?' Actually, Jay had told me once that his dad was thinking the grass was greener somewhere else. Oh, man. What a fool!

Mrs. Murphy kept working my cock with her mouth. Up and down and all around she licked. I was starting to lose control. She must have sensed it because she pulled her mouth away and began kissing up to my stomach. Then, she lifted herself up and reached over me. She opened the drawer of her nightstand and pulled something out. She closed the drawer and handed me a condom in a bright, yellow wrapper. "Saddle up," she said to me.

I wasted no time. I ripped open the bright, yellow wrapper only to find an equally bright, yellow condom inside. I set quickly to the task of putting it on and then I looked at her like I was a dog who had just heard the Pavlovian bell. She pushed me onto my back and straddled me all in one motion. She grabbed my cock and lowered herself on to it slowly.

In unison, we both emitted a long, satisfying groan of pleasure. She looked into my eyes and said, "When you get there, don't hold back."

She planted her hands on my chest and began moving her hips back and forth against my blood-engorged cock. She closed her eyes and her head fell back. Her movements against my body quickened. Her mouth fell open and she released a sharp "ah" with every thrust. Her movements quickened again and became harder. "Oh fuck," she said. Her head dropped forward and our eyes met. She smiled at me, but it wasn't one of those happy smiles. It was one of those dirty, bad-girl smiles that said, 'That's right. I'm fucking you.' That was it for me. My dick began to swell with the strongest orgasm I'd had to date. She must've felt it because she started grinding harder against me and said, "Let me have it." Hell, I had no choice. My dick erupted and I shot what I'm sure was a tank-full of come. My pulsating cock must have triggered her orgasm as well. She tossed her head back and began screaming, "Here it comes again." Her body froze. I continued to pump with what little strength I had left. Again, the little tremors returned before she completely relaxed and collapsed on top of me. We laid there for what seemed like hours, grinding slowly in our wetness before she finally pulled herself off of me and headed for the bathroom.

A few seconds later I heard the toilet flush. Then, I heard the shower come to life. A moment passed before she appeared in the doorway and said, "Come on. Shower time."

The shower with Mrs. Murphy was heavenly. We soaped each other up and washed each other down. Her clean, white skin glistened under the warm stream of water. Sunlight poured in through the shower window and highlighted the contrast of my brown skin against her. We kissed and caressed each other for quite some time before we hopped out, toweled off and were dressed once again.

I was downstairs in the living room again when she brought me the box of football equipment for which I had come. She handed it to me and we walked towards the front door. She opened it for me and I stepped through.

"Dee." she called to me.

I turned to her.

"That was real nice. Honest."

A huge smile graced me lips. "I enjoyed it, too, Mrs. Murphy."

She grinned. "This stays between me and you, okay?"

"Who would I tell?"

"I don't know. Your mother, friends at school, Jay?"

"No way," I promised. "Besides, if Jay found out, I wouldn't even know what to say."

Mrs. Murphy smiled and leaned forward. "Say...now we're even." She winked at me again and said, "See ya, Tiger." Then, she closed the door.

SPLIT DECISIONS

By
R. Daniels

ONE

Rosa's legs trembled as they tightened around Everett's thin waist. Normally, sweat would have been beading down between her large, firm breasts after having an orgasm like that. But not today. Today, sex with Everett was like it had been for the last six months or so. Sure, it was sex with love, caring and intimacy, but it was sex that somehow had become misplaced and without mutual foundation. Rosa knew it. So did he.

Rosa's legs stopped shaking. Her whole body was wrapped around Everett's, lean, muscular frame. She stared into the mirror as a tear fell from her eye and landed on Everett's shoulder. He reacted and tried to look into her eyes but she resisted and held on tighter.

"Rosa?" He spoke softly. "What's wrong, baby?"

She wiped her eyes, but didn't respond.

"Rosa?" he repeated.

Still, no response. Suddenly, Rosa untangled herself from Everett's naked body and lifted herself off his still hard penis. *'He didn't come'*, she thought. That was odd. Lately, she barely had to touch him and he was spewing his load everywhere. She knew the reason. Ever since Rosa dropped the bomb about her parents' adamant refusal to accept him, and her surprising revelation that she wasn't sure if she loved him enough to stick around, his nerves had been shot.

Rosa Maria Santos came from a long line of proud, California-raised Mexicans. Her family made frequent trips to Hermosillo to visit relatives and to keep traditional values strong and in the present. The last thing her parents wanted was for Rosa to marry a gringo. Since the day Everett began to speak of marriage, Rosa's parents began dictating to her the boundaries of the Santos marital traditions and the consequence of being disassociated from the family if she stepped outside of them. The simple fact that she now considered leaving the man she had loved for five years made her question if she ever truly loved him at all.

"I'm okay," she said as she retrieved her yellow panties from the floor. He pulled her close as she tried to push him aside and walk by. "Everett. I have to go the bathroom."

Everett looked into her big, brown eyes. He could see the conflict and confusion that danced inside her mind. If only she would let him in and allow him to be part of the solution, not the problem. "You know I love you, don't you?" He asked in an almost pleading tone.

Her expression clouded with sadness. "It's the only thing I do know." Gently, she pulled herself free of his grasp, walked into the bathroom and closed the door.

Rosa stared at the walls as she sat and relieved her bladder. What was she going to do? Her parents made it very clear that Everett was not the man they were going to allow her to marry. "He doesn't even have a career," her mother had said. "If he's such a good writer, why hasn't he published anything yet? How is he going to support you?" The questions kept coming, and Rosa knew that every single objection her parents threw at her only danced around the real issue at hand. "He's a whitey," her father had said to her. "A poor whitey at that. You want to marry someone, you marry a Mexican."

"But he loves me," Rosa protested to them time and time again. Her mother never even flinched, "Yeah, but he didn't at first. Forget him. Find someone else and move on."

Rosa stood and flushed the toilet. She washed hands her then wiped her eyes. She didn't want Everett to see her crying. She needed to project an air of indifference as best she could. Maybe then he would get tired of being treated like a dirty little secret and just leave on his own. She didn't want to have to do the hard work of breaking it off and looking like the bad guy. Was that selfishness? Vanity? Probably. The problem was, Rosa wasn't sure if she wanted him to stay or go. She did, however, know that she didn't want to be the one to break his heart.

She slid into her panties and stared at herself in the mirror. She touched her breasts. They were still a bit sensitive from the previous bout of sex. Could she get used to someone else's touch after being with Everett for so long? She took a deep breath. She knew she could; in fact, she had. Ever since she'd been contemplating the break-up, other men had started to look really good to her. Then she met Roberto.

Roberto was Ana's roommate. Ana was Rosa's co-worker, good friend and confidante. One night about six months ago, when Rosa was trying to put a little space between herself and Everett, she went out with Ana and ended up in Ana's apartment. That's where she met Roberto. He was handsome, career-minded, financially stable, single and Hispanic. Just what the Santos-family doctor ordered. It only made matters worse when she found out that Roberto was interested in her. Over the next few months, she found herself giving Everett different excuses for why she was working late, or why she couldn't be reached on her cell phone while she was out with Ana. Everett began to ask questions like, "When did you start hanging out with Ana so much?" and "How come you never invite me to go out with you and Ana?" No matter how innocent Rosa tried to make it sound, she knew it wasn't about her co-worker. It was about Roberto. Unfortunately, Everett was no fool. He knew something other than her parents' interference was brewing. Rosa tried to get him off the subject. With the situation already looking dire due to her parents, the last thing she wanted to tell him was that someone else had caught her eye. This was just one more reason why she doubted her love for him.

Rosa opened the door and exited the bathroom. Everett had already dressed and was standing in front of the window, looking out at the passing traffic on Oxnard. He turned to her. She moved to the bed and retrieved a tank top. Her firm breasts lifted and fell as she slipped the tank top over her head and onto her thick, 5'6" frame.

"I'm going to go," he said. "I'm the opening bartender tomorrow morning." He crossed the bedroom and took her in his arms. He bent and kissed her softly on the lips. "I wish you would talk to me."

"I *am* talking to you, Everett," she said, knowing it was a little white lie. "You just keep asking questions that I don't have the answers to."

"Questions like, do you love me?" he asked.

"Of course I love you," she replied.

"You just don't know if you're *in* love?" he asked.

'I'm in love', she wanted to say, *'I'm just not sure it's with you anymore.'* Rosa knew she couldn't say that to Everett, though she knew he already suspected it. Still, hearing the words would kill him, and she just wasn't prepared to come clean until she was sure she wanted to let him go, and even then, she might not tell at all. Was that cowardice? It sure was, but Rosa decided she could live with it. "I'm sorry," she finally responded. "I just need some time to figure this out."

Everett nodded. He knew time was a luxury this relationship didn't have. He turned and headed for the door. As he crossed the threshold into the hallway, she said, "I'll call you tomorrow." They both knew that she wouldn't.

TWO

Rosa sat in her cubicle and looked over the previous day's sales reports. Rosa worked in the Beverly Hills based corporate office of Hollywood Hills Fitness, Sports and Racquet Club, a franchise of health and fitness facilities that had homes in thirty-eight states across the United States. As the Regional Sales Manager, Rosa monitored the profit margin of the twenty-one clubs located within the central California region. On several occasions, Rosa had to travel to these various sites in order to implement new sales procedures, remedy any failings in the current sales practices, and keep the on-site sales managers on their toes. Needless to say, even without Mommy and Daddy Santos' money, Rosa earned a very comfortable living.

Rosa had just finished calling all of the on-site managers in her district when Ana, whose title was Regional Fitness Manager, strutted into her cubicle. Ana was a toned and fit, long-legged beauty from Guatemala. She had blonde-highlighted, silky brown hair that fell to the center of her back. Since her arrival at the corporate office eight months ago, she and Rosa had become good friends. Rosa, despite her initial decision to keep her personal life out of the workplace, found herself confiding in Ana more and more. Though Ana didn't agree with Rosa and Roberto's extra-curricular activities, she supported Rosa through her personal struggles concerning her family and Everett.

"Have you eaten lunch yet?" Ana asked through a thick, Latin accent.

"Not yet," Rosa replied. "What do you have in mind?"

"I'm thinking about a big, fat and juicy cheeseburger with fries," Ana said with a smile.

"Are you kidding me? That shit will kill you."

"Every once in a while isn't bad," Ana insisted.

Rosa gestured towards Ana. "That's because you have a body like a goddess."

"I work out every day," Ana responded, then relaxed her tone and said, "You do work in the fitness profession, Rosa. Sometimes you have to walk the walk, you know?"

Rosa glared at Ana, the woman who just invited her out for cheeseburgers. "Don't start, okay? I get preached to enough by my mother about my weight, I don't need to hear it from you, too." Rosa's cell phone began to ring. She picked it up and looked at the caller ID. "Speak of the devil." She turned back to Ana. "I'll meet you downstairs in five minutes, okay?"

"Five minutes," Ana confirmed and then exited the cubicle.

Rosa took a deep breath and answered her cell. "Hey, Mama."

"Rosita. Hi," Mama said. "I just called to see how things were going." Her tone was overly pleasant. Rosa recognized it and was immediately wary.

"A little busy, but I'm okay." *Okay, Mama. Get to it!*

"Well?" Mama began. "How did he take it?"

"Take what?" Rosa asked innocently.

"You said you were breaking up with *him*, yesterday." Mama never used Everett's name. It allowed her to ignore the fact he was a living, breathing, feeling human being. "How did he take it?"

"I didn't get a chance to do it yet," Rosa lied.

Mama Santos sighed heavily. "Rosita. You're only going to hurt the man more by prolonging it."

"Like you're really concerned about how he feels, Mama," Rosa snapped. "All you care about is what *your* friends will say when they see me with a white man. This is about you, not me." Rosa began to fume slowly.

"It's about me, huh?" Mama's voice began to increase in volume as her hot, Latin temper began to kick in. "This man can't take care of you. He has no money, Rosita, no stability. You're thirty-five years old. You're trying to tell me that that doesn't matter?"

Rosa remained quiet. Though she didn't want to admit it, Mama had a point. Rosa wanted a family of her own some day. She wanted to have a baby and raise it in a comfortable, healthy environment, one with financial stability built upon solid careers and mutual support. She knew that, in time, she could have all those things with Everett. He was a good man who truly loved her. Still, the fact remained that she was thirty-five years old. Her clock was ticking and she wanted to start building that life *now*. Everett, despite the fact that she loved him, was currently not the man for the job. Rosa began to cry. "I gotta go, Mama."

Mama knew she had upset Rosa. Distressing her oldest daughter was never her intention, but she had to make Rosa see that leaving her boyfriend was the best possible decision she could make. Mama knew about Roberto but felt this was not the time to press that particular issue. "Rosa, listen. The sooner you do it, the better."

Rosa retorted sharply, "Yes, Mama. I know. Okay?"

Mama's tone relaxed. "Call me later."

"Fine," Rosa said and disconnected the call. She threw the phone down on the desk and buried her face in her hands. 'Why can't she just get off my back about this?' she asked herself. She knew her mother was never going to allow her to be happy as long as she stayed with Everett. She found herself torn between what she knows she should do- fight for the man she loves and don't give up, - and what she feels she wants to do, -get free and start all over again without disappointing the family. At the moment, she wasn't especially fond of either choice. One way or another, someone was going to lose.

THREE

Rosa came home from work exhausted. Between constant reiteration of proper sales procedures to her on-site managers and arguing with her mother, she was ready to make herself an Absolut Martini with bleu cheese-stuffed olives and call it a night. Rosa kicked off her shoes before going into the kitchen and mixing the drink She grabbed a pack of light cigarettes before moving into the living room and making a comfortable landing on her sofa. She flicked her lighter and ignited the cancer stick. She didn't know how many times she'd promised herself she was going to kick the habit, but it was probably as many times as she had told herself she'd smoke *just one more pack* before giving them up for good. Rosa sucked down half the martini in one gulp. God, it tasted good. Who cares if one gram of alcohol is equivalent to seven empty calories? She didn't. There was no way in the world she wanted to hear that alcohol consumption destroyed any and every diet she'd tried over the last year. When Rosa wanted a drink, that's all that mattered. And what Rosa Santos wants, Rosa Santos gets. Ana had laughed at her once and said, "I swear you're the Latin version of a Jewish-American Princess." Rosa always shrugged off the comment, but lately, she began to wonder if it was true.

Rosa had only taken three drags from her cigarette when there was a knock at the door. She sighed heavily as she made her way across the living room and pulled the door open. It was Everett. She tried to smile, but all she really wanted was to be left alone. Everett sensed it immediately.

"Hey," she said, trying to sound excited to see him.

"Hey," he replied solemnly. "I know I should have called first but I didn't want you to talk me out of coming over."

"I wouldn't have done that." She lied. He knew it.

He took a breath and held out his hand. Resting in his open palm was a small red box. "I got this from someone selling little trinkets in front of that Psychic shop on Ventura Boulevard."

"What is it?" she asked with a mixture of genuine concern and subtle indifference.

"Open it," he said.

Rosa took the small red box and pulled off the cover. All the while, Everett, realizing she had no intention of inviting him inside, stood and watched silently.

Rosa reached into the box and pulled out a silver plated wishbone. "It's like the kind that you get out of the turkey on Thanksgiving," he explained.

"How sweet," she said. When Rosa and Everett first began dating, Everett would always bring her little tokens of affection. Quite often, he would buy these items while she was away on business and surprise her with it upon her return. It had been some time since he had bought her something like this, and considering how she'd been feeling about him lately, she felt slightly guilty accepting it.

"I know it isn't much, but it made me think of you and all the things we used to wish for together," he explained, knowing she wasn't nearly as excited about the gift as she would've been a year earlier.

A look of sadness crossed her face. "Everett," she said.

"It's okay," he interrupted. "I'm going to go. I just wanted to give you that." He smiled. "The guy I bought it from advised me to use it wisely. He said to hold it over your heart, but to be careful what you wish for."

"Thank you," she said with sincerity.

Everett shifted his weight from one leg to another as he stood in the hallway. He shrugged slightly and broke the silence. "Okay, uh, I'm gonna go. I'll call you tomorrow." He leaned forward and kissed her on the lips. He looked into her eyes before turning and walking slowly down the hall.

Rosa felt horrible for not inviting him inside, but the fact was, she didn't want to. She felt bad about that, too. She truly hated causing him pain, but she simply didn't know what to do.

—

"He's a good guy, Rosa," Ana said to her as they spoke on the phone later. "I can't believe you're walking away from a guy who loves you, I mean *really* loves you."

Rosa stretched as she rested supine on her queen-sized bed. "You forget that he didn't want this relationship at first," Rosa responded.

"My God, Rosa. You act like you've never dated a man before. None of them want it in the beginning," Ana said with a laugh. "Sure, they want it long enough to get into your pants, but then they act like they don't want everything that goes along with it."

"Well, if you understand that, why are you giving me such a hard time?"

"Because I understand *men*, Chica. They never want the relationship once the honeymoon phase is over. They're too stupid to know that they want it. It's just not in their nature to commit right away." Ana laughed. "Believe me. He hasn't been sticking around for nothing."

"He knows I want out," Rosa protested. "Now he's just scared to lose me."

"Maybe he is," Ana conceded. "But a scared man who doesn't love you would've bailed by now, especially with all the shit you're putting him through."

"What am I putting him through?"

"For starters, the resistance from your family," Ana replied. "I'm sure it doesn't make him feel good to know your family won't accept him."

"And that's my fault?"

"No, but it doesn't help that you haven't stood up for him," Ana said. "Not to mention, you told him that you're uncertain about being in love with him. And let's not forget Roberto."

"He doesn't know about Roberto," Rosa assured her.

"You keep telling yourself that, Rosa. Everett may not know Roberto's name or who he is, but he knows he's not getting the whole truth."

"I just don't want to hurt him," Rosa said sincerely.

"I know, but...you are. Trust me, Rosa. Whether he's afraid of losing you or not, the man loves you."

Rosa picked up the silver-plated wishbone that Everett had given her earlier. She held it by the long end and rolled it back and forth between her fingers. "I don't know, Ana. What about all the shit he's put me through? What about the girl he dated when he broke up with me three years ago. When he came to his senses and came back to me, I lived with the fact that he had trouble getting over her."

"But it was your choice to stay and he did eventually get over her." Ana sighed.

"What about all the other times he broke up with me because he didn't know what he wanted?" Rosa continued to question.

Ana sighed. "Look, I'm not dismissing any of that but it sounds like he's honestly trying to make up for it." Her tone softened. "There comes a point where you have to let the past and all the bad grudges go, you know? Hell, if my ex-husband loved me half as much as Everett loves you, I'd still be married."

"Wasn't he cheating on you?" Rosa asked.

Ana thought for a minute. "Oh yeah. You're right. But I'm sure he learned, as you soon might, that the grass isn't always greener."

"Maybe not, but I need some space to figure out what I really want, you know? I'm so tired of trying to please everyone, and I really want to."

"I know you do," Ana said. "Unfortunately, you might have to make a decision that's going to tear you apart. I know it's not easy, but..." Ana's voice trailed off. Suddenly, she chuckled and said, "Now, if there were two of you..."

Rosa laughed. "Oh, I wish there were. That would make life so much easier. I could have my parents and Roberto in one hand, and work on things with Everett in the other."

Ana's tone became serious. "Yeah, but is that what you want? To please everyone but yourself?"

"Oh, I'd be pleased. Trust me," Rosa assured her again. "The only problem I'd have is deciding which one of me would go to work." They laughed. Ana spent the next hour listening to Rosa and giving her advice. Still, when they said goodbye for the night, Rosa was as confused as ever before. Her mind raced as she thought about her situation and how she ended up in the middle of it. *'Someone was going to lose'*, she thought as she drifted off to sleep. She didn't want it to be Rosa Santos.

—

Friday morning took its time coming. Rosa opened her eyes and stared at the glowing green numbers of the clock radio. 5:30 am. She had been asleep for seven and a half hours. She felt like she had been sleeping for days. 'It must have been the martinis', she thought to herself. At least she didn't have a hangover. She ran her fingers through her hair and sat upright. She glanced to her right and stared at her reflection in the mirror next to the bed. After a second, she remembered there was no mirror next to the bed.

Rosa screamed and leapt to the floor. She turned and froze in place. She couldn't believe her eyes. There, standing on the other side of the bed, was a woman who looked exactly like her. Same dark hair, same firm breasts, same thick and curvy frame. "What the fuck?" they said in unison. Instinctively, Rosa glanced at the object in her hand. She was holding what appeared to be half of the silver-plated wishbone. She looked across the bed. The other Rosa was holding the other half. Suddenly, Everett's words from the night before rang clearly in both of their minds, 'Be careful what you wish for.'

Though they didn't want to believe it, Rosa had gotten her wish. Now, there were two of them.

FOUR

"Oh, God!" Rosa exclaimed. "Please tell me I'm dreaming."

The other Rosa's jaw dropped. The reality of the situation began to set in. "I don't think we are," she said as she stared at her counterpart. She held up her half of the wishbone and asked, "What the fuck did Everett do to me?"

Rosa shook her head in disbelief, all the while eyeing the doppelganger that stood before her. She opened her mouth to speak but no words came out.

The other Rosa moved suddenly towards the phone. "I'm going to call him."

Rosa launched herself towards the bed. In an effort to retrieve the phone first, Rosa grabbed her double's wrist. Both Rosas jumped back. The physical contact made the situation eerily tangible. Rosa calmed herself and looked at her new twin. "No. We can't call him."

"Why not? He did this to us."

"No. I did it when I wished there were two of us," Rosa recalled.

The other Rosa put her hands on her hips and glared into Rosa's eyes. "What do you mean *you* did it? *I* made the wish."

"No, I did, last night-"

"-talking to Ana," they said in unison. The Rosas' gasped and fell silent. Their eyes widened as another realization took hold. They were both claiming to be the sole Rosa Santos that existed the night before, which only led them to another unsettling revelation. The wish didn't merely make a double of Rosa Santos, the wish literally split her in two. It made no sense to argue about which Rosa was the original since it was obvious that both were entitled to the claim. Finally, after several moments of silence, Rosa spoke. "What are we going to do?"

Initially, the other Rosa looked perplexed. As far as she knew, this was an unprecedented experience. Then, a grin began to form along her mouth and eventually swelled into a full-on smile. "We're going to do what we said we'd do. Have our cake and eat it, too."

—

It took little over an hour for the Rosas to come up with a plan of action to deal with their present life situation. First, they decided that it was way too confusing to keep calling each other Rosa, so one of them took the moniker of Rosie. Then, after much deliberation, they decided that calling in sick sounded more appealing than choosing which of them should sit at a desk for eight hours. Neither of them would be able to concentrate on work anyway.

Rosie volunteered happily to go see Everett. "We can have a fresh start," she said gleefully. "No more lies, just us, working together to make this relationship strong."

Rosa didn't seem fazed in the slightest. "Fine. He *is* a good guy and I suppose he deserves a real chance with you."

Rosie turned to her. "You suppose?"

"Yeah," Rosa answered. "It's funny. I feel nothing for him."

"Nothing?" Rosie was troubled slightly by Rosa's revelation, to think that a part of her felt nothing for a man who loved her completely. Though they were now split, Rosa was still a part of who she is, or at least, was.

"Nope," Rosa said quickly. "That is what we wanted, right?"

Rosie thought for a moment, and then smiled weakly. "Yeah. I guess so."

Rosa laughed. "Wow. A part of me was still in love with Everett. Who would've imagined?"

"So," Rosie began, "when are you leaving?" The girls had decided that Rosa was going to fly north to San Francisco for the weekend and announce her newfound freedom to her parents.

"As soon as I get dressed, I'll go to LAX and see if I can catch a flight out this afternoon," Rosa explained. "It will be nice to have a conversation with Mama and Papa without them hounding me to leave

Everett."

"Amen to that," Rosie said before rushing into the bathroom. "Have fun. I'm going to go show Everett the time of his life." The bathroom door slammed behind her.

Rosa went to the phone and set herself to the task of making airline reservations. She and Rosie had discussed her return to Los Angeles on early Monday morning, but Rosa decided she was going to come back late Sunday night. Roberto will be so surprised.

—

Rosie barely gave Everett time to react to her sudden appearance at the door before launching herself at him and wrapping her arms around his body.

Everett grinned from ear to ear. "What's going on, baby?" Everett looked into her eyes. For the first time in months, he saw a sparkle of love and caring. He brushed a stray lock of dark hair from her face and caressed her cheeks. "Is this really happening?" he questioned.

Rosie looked up at Everett and ran her hand through his curly, brown hair. "I'm sorry," she said. "I never want to hurt you again. I love you so much. Let's start over, okay? Let's learn from our mistakes and grow from them together."

"Can we?" he asked skeptically.

"I think so. I hope so."

Everett smiled. "Do you mean it?"

"I do," she said.

"What about your parents?" he asked.

Rosie smiled. "Don't worry. Rosa's taking care of them." Everett began to laugh. 'It had been quite some time since she'd heard his laughter,' she thought. *I guess it's been a while since he had anything to be happy about.* Rosie pushed the thought from her mind. She stepped forward and forced Everett backwards into his apartment. "Now," she said, "let me take care of you."

—

Candlelight flickered and cast dancing shadows on their naked bodies as they stood, embracing each other, in the middle of the bedroom. A puddle of clothing was draped around their feet. Rosie pressed her lips against Everett's. His hands slid down the length of her back and caressed her thick, round ass. He squeezed her plump bottom and pulled her closer. Rosie stood on the tips of her toes, allowing Everett to reach beyond her glorious buttocks and insert his middle finger into her wetness. She moaned and pressed her lips even harder into his mouth.

Everett stepped forward, causing Rosie to backpedal towards the bed. She giggled as she tried to maintain her balance while keeping Everett's probing finger deep inside her dripping pussy. He tried to push her onto the mattress. Rosie resisted him. She pulled away and spun them around in place, positioning Everett in front of the bed. He complied without struggle. She forced him backwards and climbed on top of him as he landed on the queen-sized bed. The full impact of her compact, 180 lb frame came down on Everett. He smiled. He loved the feel of her weight on him, the flow of her hair as it fell onto his neck and the touch of her hands as she stroked his body up and down. The sensation of her nipples tickling his skin as she pressed her full breasts against his chest caused his throbbing penis to become even harder.

She bore her tongue into the flesh of his neck before kissing a path up to his mouth. Everett wrapped his strong arms around her and held her tight. Their wet kisses echoed as their combined passion began to escalate. Everett moved his hands to her face and began placing kisses from one side of her face to the other. Rosie released a soft sigh. She hadn't realized how much she missed those facial kisses, one of the little things that she took for granted before the split from Rosa. "Oh, Everett!" she exclaimed passionately. In response, Everett lifted his weight and rolled her onto her back. She maneuvered herself under him as he mounted her and began sucking feverishly on her round, protruding nipples. His soft tongue licked around her areola, sending sharp ripples of warmth down to the pleasure center between her legs. Everett alternated between her breasts several times before starting his descent toward her nether region. Rosie stopped him. He looked up into her eyes.

"No," she said with bated breath. "I need you inside me." Everett's hard-on went into overdrive.

He reversed his direction and positioned himself over her. His pulsating member had no trouble finding her puffy, pink pussy lips and parting them. Everett stared into her dark eyes as he pushed his cock into her hot wetness. Rosie threw her arms to her sides and surrendered to the feeling of having Everett's manhood deep inside her. Their eyes remained locked on each other as he began to pump his meat repeatedly into her hungry canal. She raised her legs and threw them around his back. "That's right. Get in there," she said as he plunged even deeper and filled her completely with every thrust.

Rosie reached up and grabbed his shoulders. She locked her legs around his thighs and arched her back. She began to rub her clit against his dick as he, again and again, pumped into her. Everett wrapped his arms around her round ass and pushed harder. Rosie emitted a throaty moan of delight. He had found the spot. Waves of hot pleasure raced through her body as her climax began to form. Everett quickened the pace. He closed his eyes as he became lost in the feeling. "No," Rosie said. "Look at me," she demanded as her orgasm began to build within her.

Everett opened his eyes. He accelerated his pace once more and began to moan aloud.

Small knots began to form deep within Rosie. She was close. Everett knew she was on the brink of climax and ground his penis against the roof of her pussy. "Omigod, omigod, omigod," she began to repeat as the knots inside of her released suddenly and sent a cascade of warm orgasmic sensation throughout her body. Everett continued to thrust into her as he squeezed her tighter. Rosie's body shuddered and hot sweat formed on her skin as her climax enveloped her. Everett continued to push his cock into her, wanting her to get every bit of pleasure possible.

He rubbed harder against the roof of her pussy once again. Rosie shook as the aftershocks from her orgasm triggered yet another climactic release. "Omigod, Everett, omigod, oh shit, don't stop, don't stop." Everett obeyed happily. They moved together in perfect rhythm until her orgasmic tremors subsided and her body began to relax. Their eyes remained locked on each other the entire time.

Rosie surmised that Everett had gotten control of his nerves because his cock was still rock-hard inside of her. 'I know how to fix that,' she thought to herself. She unwrapped her legs from around his body and starting pushing him away.

"Where are you going?" he asked playfully, resisting her.

"I want to feel you come inside me," she said.

He smiled. It had been quite sometime since she was so eager to have his juices fill her. "I will. Let me enjoy this for a while," he begged.

"Oh, you will. Trust me." She pushed at him again. He released her and rolled aside. Rosie turned over and planted herself on her elbows and knees. She lowered her head and arched her back so her beautiful, round ass was protruding high into the air. "Just the way you like it."

Everett grinned from ear to ear. "You know me well," he said as he maneuvered behind her and pushed his throbbing cock into her. 'Doggie-style,' he thought to himself. 'Canines have no idea how good they have it.'

Everett began to pump into her. Rosie crossed her arms and rested her head against them. She wanted to stabilize herself so Everett could go full throttle without pushing her over.

Everett grabbed her hips and began to thrust wildly into her from behind. Oh, how he loved the feeling of her full, round ass-cheeks as they slapped back against his body. Everett was certain there wasn't a more perfect ass walking the planet. He loved her ass so much, that if he wasn't so busy fucking her from behind, he would bend down and lick her ass from stem to stern. He loved this woman beyond measure and there was nothing he wouldn't do to show it.

He closed his eyes. He knew if he looked at her ass while he was hammering away, he would shoot his load right then and there. He didn't know why, but there was something about seeing her firm ass ripple against his thrusts that sent him over the edge. Then again, maybe it was the heart-shape her ass formed when she was bent over like that. He wasn't sure, but he knew it drove him crazy.

Rosie released her arms and lowered her hips onto the bed slowly. Everett followed and continued to move in and out of her even as she laid flat on the mattress. "Let me have it, baby," she said to him. "Don't move. Just let me have it."

Everett thrust his cock deeply into her pussy. He reached down and parted her plump ass cheeks so he could bury himself as far as he possibly could. Then, he placed his palms on the bed and held himself there, motionless. Slowly, Rosie grabbed at his pulsating cock with her pussy. She increased the pace gradually, rubbing her ass against his body as her pussy grabbed harder and harder at his dick.

"Oh, yeah, Rosa," he said aloud.

"That's it, baby," she said. "Let it go. Give it to me." Rosie arched her back slightly and gripped his dick with every ounce of strength her pussy muscles could muster. It only took a few strokes before Everett screamed. His body shook above her as his penis jerked and shot jism deep within her. The warm fluid filled her and sparked another climax inside of her. Within seconds, they were coming together and screaming in harmonic ecstasy.

After a few moments, Everett collapsed on top of her. He wrapped his arms around her and kissed the back of her neck. "That was incredible," he said.

She giggled. "Wild and crazy. Just like old times."

"I guess all it took was knowing that you still desired me, you know, that being with me sexually still did it for you," Everett said, and then kissed her neck again.

"I was kind of confused for a little while," she said. "I'm sorry."

"It's in the past now," he said. "I love you, Rosa, my beautiful Latin Rose."

"I love you, too," she said.

"Nothing is going to get in the way of our happiness from now on," he promised. "Nothing."

Rosie smiled and snuggled into the weight of his body. It wasn't long before they were both fast asleep, dreaming of things to come.

—

So far, Rosa's weekend in San Francisco was worry free. The family had come together when Rosa announced she was flying in suddenly with some important news. It didn't take long for the Santos family grapevine to transmit the info to her siblings and other family members that Rosa had finally disposed of her gringo boyfriend.

Her younger brother, Pablo, who, after three years of classes at the University of Phoenix was still no closer to completing an eighteen month program, dropped everything and jumped into his car to be there. Pablo couldn't care one way or the other who Rosa dated, he just liked being in the thick of things when any type of drama arose. Rosa's sister, Noemi, who lived in Florida with her very successful Hispanic-lawyer-husband had flown in the day before with said husband in tow. Though Rosa wouldn't admit it, she was envious of Noemi, who, at ten years her junior, had managed to land a husband, a Latino no less, and buy a beautiful $150,000 home that would surely sell for almost four times that amount in California. "And I was wasting time with Everett," Rosa said to herself. "What was I thinking?"

Mama was simply overjoyed that Rosa had decided to come to her senses and let Everett go. "It's for the best," Mama assured her. "You'll see."

"He would have never fit in," her father added as he crossed into the living room from the kitchen and sat in his recliner. Papa had just finished eating a large Mexican meal and was now ready to engage in his favorite after-dinner activity. *La siesta.* "Le hiciste favor al chico," he said in Spanish. "Now you can concentrate on finding a nice Hispanic husband, one who isn't working for tips or some shit like that."

"Alright," Rosa snapped while trying not to seem annoyed. She calmed her tone. "Let it go already." Although Rosa felt she was no longer in love with Everett, she still cared enough for him to abhor hearing their negative opinions about him. *'Fuck'*, she thought. *'It's not like any of you ever took the time to even meet him.'* Rosa caught herself. 'Why am I still defending him?' she wondered in silence. 'I left him so I could put all of this behind me and stop fighting with my parents.' Rosa shook her head as if she could literally jar the thoughts of Everett from her mind. It wasn't long before she allowed the comfort of home and the chatter of family and friends to divert her attention.

Saturday morning, Mama took Rosa and Noemi on a shopping spree. Mama loved having her girls around and enjoyed spoiling them and making sure they had whatever they wanted or needed. They spent hours in the shoe store, rummaging through and trying on countless styles and colors. Rosa enjoyed this time with Mama. It made her forget about all the pressures of life-a job, bills to pay, relationships. There was nothing like a day just for the girls. The outing would have been absolutely perfect had they not started trying on clothes in the department store. Mama watched as Rosa squeezed into a pair of jeans. "I don't understand how you work for a fitness club and can't seem to lose weight," she said. Rosa knew Mama didn't mean those words as harshly as they sounded, but it hurt Rosa just the same.

"It's not like I work in the actual club, Mama," Rosa responded. "Besides, it's hard to stick to a diet when I'm always traveling."

"Can't you ask your job to keep you at home more often?" Mama asked.

"I'm the Regional Manager, Mama. It's part of my job description."

"It must be tough having a job that takes you away from your life so often," Noemi said. "I'm sure that must have been tough on your relationship with Everett."

Here we go. Everett again. "My traveling wasn't the reason Everett and I had problems."

"Well, I'm sure it didn't help," Noemi said innocently.

"You know what doesn't help?" Rosa snapped. "People not knowing how to stay out of my business, that's what doesn't help. It's over, okay? I left him. Can we just drop it now?" Rosa walked to the dressing room door and opened it. Before stepping through, she turned to Mama and said, "And I'll take the jeans." Rosa exited the dressing room. Mama and Noemi exchanged a quick glance before breaking into laughter. No one made an exit like Rosa.

Later that evening, the family was scattered around the house after dinner. Rosa found herself lounging in Papi's recliner as she nursed her third glass of red wine. Renita, a long-time friend of Mama's, came and sat on the sofa next to her.

"Hey, chica," she greeted Rosa. "How are you?"

"I'm good. And you?"

"Hanging in there," Renita responded. "I heard about your important decision."

Rosa sighed. "Why is everyone making such a big deal out of it?"

"Maybe because it is a big deal," Renita said, attempting to sound comforting. "Are you sure this is what you want?"

"I think it's for the best," Rosa responded.

"Yeah?" Renita questioned. "Isn't this the same guy you've been trying to get to commit to you for the last three and a half years?"

Rosa nodded.

"And now that he's trying to work things out with you, you leave him?"

"He waited a bit too long, Renita," Rosa responded.

"It seems kind of pointless to walk away from something you've been working so hard for just as you're about to get it." Renita said. Rosa remained quiet. Almost every time she had come home in the past, she confided in Renita about how much she wished Everett would get beyond whatever it was that kept him from committing to her and love her completely. At the time, she wasn't concerned that her family didn't approve, she just wanted Everett to wake up and see the light. Renita had always been supportive and encouraged Rosa to hold on to her love, despite the opposition from her parents. "Are you sure there isn't something else going on?" Renita asked.

Rosa looked at Renita but said nothing. Fortunately, she didn't have to. Renita could see the conflict in Rosa's eyes. She placed her hand on

Rosa's and smiled. "If you ever need to talk, I'm here."

"Thank you," Rosa said gratefully.

Renita squeezed Rosa's hand before standing and leaving Rosa alone in the living room.

Rosa appreciated all of Renita's support over the last three years, but she was convinced that she had made the right decision. Besides, her situation with Rosie had made it easy. She couldn't have asked for a better way out.

—

Rosie and Everett stayed in bed most of the weekend. Except for quick runs to the kitchen and bathroom, they made love and cuddled in Everett's bed through early Sunday morning. After another passionate session of marathon lovemaking, they, again, feel asleep in each other's arms. Around noon, Rosie was awakened by the sensation of Everett's tongue stroking her clit lightly. She moaned her approval as he wrapped his arms around the top of her thighs and buried his tongue inside of her. It wasn't long before her senses were overwhelmed and she reached another earth-shattering climax.

After the sensations subsided, Everett remained between her legs and licked her pink lips gently. Rosie thought nothing could take away from this perfect moment, that is, until the phone rang. Once, twice, three times...

"You gonna answer that?" she asked.

"No," he said as he ran his tongue across her clit once again. "Let the machine get it."

A few seconds passed before the answering machine picked up. Everett's brief outgoing message outlined his requests to insure a prompt return call before the machine beeped and recorded the incoming information. "Everett, this is Stephen. Janet called in sick and we're short a bartender tonight. I would definitely owe you one if you could fill in. Give me a call. Thanks." The message ended and the phone disconnected the call.

An unexpected chill ran up Rosie's spine. She placed her hands on the bed and squirmed away from Everett's probing tongue.

"What's wrong?" he asked.

"Don't you think you should go to work?" she asked in response.

"No. I want to stay here with you."

"Yeah, but you could use the money, right?"

"Yeah, but, I'm sure I could miss a day."

Rosie sat up and reached for her panties. "No," she said. "If you have a chance to make money, then you should."

"I don't care about the money, Rosa. It's no big deal," he said, feeling confused. "What's up? Don't you want to spend the day with me?" he asked with a smile.

"Of course I do," she forced herself to say. She stood by the bed and had her panties on before Everett could move to her side to try and stop her.

"Then why are you running away?" he asked.

"I'm not," she said. The truth was, the phone call from Everett's boss made her remember that Everett was still living paycheck to paycheck. He was, in no way, capable of providing her the kind of life she dreamed of, one supported by assured financial stability. As she strapped on her bra, she tried to shake the thoughts from her brain. *'What's going on?'* she asked herself silently. *'Rosa is supposed to be feeling these things. Not me.'* She turned to Everett. She could see the look of worry spreading across his face. She stepped closer to him and caressed his face with her palm. "Just go to work," she said calmly. "I feel like I've kept you from your life all weekend."

"You're part of my life," he said.

She looked into his eyes and met his gaze. She hoped and prayed that he didn't see the doubts and insecurities resurfacing behind her dark pupils. His expression let her know that he did. Slowly, he dropped his head and stared at the floor. He knew that whatever it was that inspired her to come back to him this weekend had once again retreated. Though she was standing right in front of him, he felt alone.

He turned away, disappointed, and headed for the bathroom. "I guess I better get ready for work."

"I'm sorry," she said weakly.

"What else is new?" he muttered, barely audible.

The bathroom door closed. Rosie stood there, transfixed. Though she felt horrible about disappointing Everett, she was more concerned with the sudden onrush of adverse feelings towards him. Feelings she thought only Rosa had.

—

Rosa sat on the couch in Roberto and Ana's apartment. She had called Roberto as soon as her plane landed at LAX. She couldn't wait to give him the news. She had officially ended her relationship with Everett and she was all his. He sounded ecstatic on the phone. In person, however, he was as cool as a cucumber.

Ana made a discreet exit as soon as Rosa arrived. Roberto offered her a glass of wine and joined her on the sofa. He asked her the usual questions about her break-up with Everett, 'How do you feel?', 'What did he say?', 'Are you okay?', all of the standard queries to ascertain where he, now, does or doesn't fit in.

After a long conversation, Roberto went into the kitchen to whip up a quick meal. He put a pot of water on the stove and stood there as if he was waiting for it to boil. Rosa decided she wasn't going to wait a moment longer. After having to sneak around and lie for so long just to see him, she wasn't going to let anything else get in her way. After all, what Rosa Santos wants, Rosa Santos gets.

She marched into the kitchen and threw her arms around him. She pulled him close and pushed her tongue into his mouth. She felt his immediate, involuntary response pressing against her. She grabbed at the opening of his shirt and pulled in opposite directions. Several buttons popped and cascaded across the kitchen tile. She began kissing his chest and biting his nipples wildly. He reached down and unbuttoned her tight jeans. He yanked at the zipper and revealed the nude-colored thong within. She grabbed the top of her jeans and pulled them down, unleashing her round, firm ass and thick thighs. As her jeans dropped to her ankles, she repeated the same action with her thong. Within seconds, she was kicking them out from under her feet.

Roberto wasted no time discarding his slacks and underwear. His hard-on sprang out in front of him as he stood and began manipulating the harness on Rosa's nude colored bra. In no time, they were both naked, standing in the kitchen, wrapped in a passionate embrace.

Rosa fell to her knees and grabbed at Roberto's member. She opened her mouth and took him in to the back of her throat. She sucked in long, even strokes, back and forth along his engorged cock. Roberto released a groan of pleasure as she devoured him inch by inch. Suddenly, she released his tool and ran her tongue down the length of his scrotum, past his balls to the small spot right below. "Oh, shit!' he exclaimed as she tickled him with her tongue. She moved in reverse and stopped at his nuts, licking each one quickly and gently before traveling back up the length of his penis and taking him into her hot mouth once again. She grunted as she sucked feverishly on his manhood, taking in the full length of it with each and every stroke.

Roberto reached down and pulled Rosa from her knees. He kissed her lips hungrily, tasting the warmth from his own cock in her mouth. He backed her up against the counter and pushed aside the envelopes and bills that were scattered there. Rosa reached back and pulled herself up. Once seated on the counter, she parted her legs, revealing her steaming, hot pink pussy-lips. She sucked on her middle finger before rubbing it across her clit and parting the pink folds that guarded her aching joybox. She inserted a finger, all the while staring at Roberto while he retrieved a condom from his wallet and rolled it down his cock quickly.

He stepped forward and pulled Rosa's hips to the edge of the counter. She spread her legs wider and wrapped them around his waist as the head of his penis parted her lips and penetrated her wet canal. Rosa released a moan and pulled Roberto as close as she could without causing herself to fall off the counter. She inserted her soaking middle finger into Roberto's mouth. He sucked ravenously, enjoying the tastes of her juices on her finger.

They began to move in rhythm as Roberto plowed deeply into her, harder and harder with each thrust. Rosa released an inarticulate utterance that coincided with the repeated smacking of his flesh against hers. "O...my...God," she stuttered. "Don't stop. Don't...stop!"

Roberto grabbed at Rosa's firm ass and held her in place as he rammed his cock into her as hard as he possibly could. He reached under her buttocks and pulled her round ass-cheeks apart. He arched his pelvis and buried every inch of his penis into her. Rosa's body tightened as her climax began to mount within her. "Oh yeah," she said. "That's it."

"Yeah?" Roberto asked breathlessly.

"Oh yeah," she managed to say.

Roberto reached behind Rosa's neck and gripped a patch of her dark hair. He tugged her tresses lightly as he continued to dig deeper into her. "Ohhh," she moaned. "Here I come. Oh, God. Don't stop!"

Rosa's body tightened as her climax began. Her legs began to shake as tiny quakes rippled through her. Roberto continued to plunge into her as she jerked about on his pulsating cock. Roberto reached his limit and his tool jumped inside of her as his balls released his hot fluid as well. They continued to moan and grind on each other, both releasing groans of satisfaction as they slowed finally to an exhausted pace. After a few moments, the only audible sounds in the kitchen were that of Rosa and Roberto's fatigued breathing, and the pot of water on the stove that had, at last, reached a steady boil.

—

It was late. Three hours had passed since Rosa's surprise appearance at the door. Ana had managed to sneak back into the apartment sometime after Roberto and Rosa had adjourned to his bedroom. Roberto lay in bed as he watched Rosa gather her clothes and get dressed.

Rosa was on cloud nine. It was nice being with Roberto without having to think about Everett. Then, just as the thought of Everett crossed her mind, she felt a familiar pang in her stomach. 'Was that guilt?' she asked herself. 'No way,' she answered. 'I have no reason to feel guilty about this at all. This is what I want and I'm not in love with Everett anymore. Right?'

She turned to Roberto, who had become unusually silent. "I'll try to leave work early tomorrow. Maybe we can get some dinner," she said.

"Tomorrow?" he asked. "Oh, uh, I was going to play ball with the guys. We've been kind of planning it for a few weeks."

"Oh," she said, disappointed. "Maybe Tuesday, then."

"Yeah," Roberto responded dismissively. "We'll talk about it tomorrow. I'll call you after the game."

'Boy,' she thought. 'That sounded an awful lot like the bullshit I've been feeding Everett for the last few months. "Okay," she said weakly, wondering why all of a sudden the guy who wanted her so desperately when she belonged to someone else, now appeared to be not so enthusiastic about having her all to himself.

Rosa crawled onto the bed and hugged Roberto tightly. She didn't know why, but she felt she had to test him. Did he caress her as if he had just struck gold, or as if he wanted her to disappear as quickly as she appeared? He wrapped his arms around her and pulled her close. She placed her head on his shoulders and exhaled slowly. She waited a second. Then, she felt it. Resistance. He seemed just a little too anxious to pull away. She squeezed a little tighter. Finally, she felt his body give in and warm up to her embrace. She held on to him for a few moments before pulling away and kissing him lovingly on the lips. She gathered her purse and looked into his eyes. "I'll call you tomorrow," she said.

"Okay," he agreed.

She kissed him again and then headed for the door. She crossed the living room and exited the apartment. Once she was inside her car, she did a quick inventory of her emotions. Happiness, fear, and guilt. The happiness came from the freedom of being with Roberto. The fear came from the unknown of what her relationship with Roberto might hold. The guilt? She couldn't explain the guilt, and she certainly didn't like what the presence of that feeling implied.

She started her car and darted into the street. She needed to get home and talk to Rosie. Something was going wrong with their plan and she had to know if Rosie was experiencing it, too.

—

"We've got problems," Rosa said as she entered the apartment and crossed into the living room. "The feelings didn't split evenly."

Rosie sat comfortably on the couch. She held a lit cigarette in one hand while she placed a vodka martini on the coffee table with the other. "Tell me about it," she responded sarcastically. "What are you doing back already?" she asked Rosa. "I thought you were coming back tomorrow."

Rosa smiled devilishly. "I came back early and surprised Roberto."

"You did what?"

"You heard me," Rosa said. "Fucked him right there in his kitchen." Rosie shook her head in disapproval. Rosa stepped towards her. "What? We did this so we could have the freedom to do what we wanted."

"Yeah, well you see how well that turned out," Rosie reminded her as she took a drag from the cigarette. "I spent the entire weekend with Everett. It was great. I didn't think about Mama once. Everything was fine until his job called and I realized that allowing myself to love him doesn't necessarily mean we'd have stability."

"I guess love just isn't enough sometimes, is it?" Rosa questioned.

Rosie shrugged. "I don't know. Maybe he's just the right guy with the wrong bank account."

"And the wrong race according to Mama," Rosa reminded her. "Don't forget that."

"Why does Mama get the last say in my happiness anyway?" Rosie asked.

"Maybe because she's family, or maybe, just maybe because we're not strong enough or mature enough to stand up to her," Rosa blurted without thinking. They exchanged glances but remained quiet. Finally, the unspoken truth had been let out of the bag. After a few painfully silent seconds, she moved and sat next to Rosie on the couch. When Rosa spoke again, her tone was soft. "You know, Roberto seemed a little different tonight."

"How so?" Rosie asked.

"I'm not sure," Rosa answered. "I figured he'd be a little more excited about the fact that I wasn't with Everett anymore."

"Maybe he doesn't know what to do with you now that he can actually have you," Rosie surmised. "They say forbidden pussy is the best pussy."

"Who says that?" Rosa asked.

Rosie shrugged. "I don't know. Somebody." She picked up the vodka martini and slurped in a mouthful. "I guess now we'll see if all the sneaking around was worth it."

"Maybe," Rosa said. "Of course, I didn't expect to feel guilty afterwards."

"I thought you didn't love Everett," Rosie questioned.

"I thought you *did*," Rosa countered.

Rosie raised her glass to Rosa before bringing it to her mouth and downing the rest of the beverage. "Touché. I guess it goes to show that even when there are two of us, we can't run from ourselves."

"So what do we do? Nothing we planned turned out exactly as we planned it."

"We do the only thing we can do," Rosie paused. "We do what's best for everyone."

"Which is?"

"Don't play dumb, Rosa," she said. "You know what we have to do. The question is, are we prepared to do it?"

Rosa exhaled heavily and looked at her double. "Yeah. I am."

"Good." Rosie stood and headed for the bedroom. ."We'll do it tomorrow, but for now, first things first." She disappeared down the short hallway and reemerged a few seconds later. In her hand, she held the silver plated wishbone given to her by Everett. To Rosa's surprise, the trinket was intact. Rosie crossed the room and held it out to Rosa, who grabbed the other end of it. Rosie took a deep breath. "Let's just hope this thing's good for one more wish."

The two women made their wish and retired immediately to the bedroom for the evening. By the time morning arrived, Rosa Santos was, again, unique.

FIVE

Eleven months had passed. Rosa checked her watch as she whisked her way through the Fashion Square Mall. It was only 7:30 pm. Good. Most of her Christmas shopping had been done but she had run out of holiday greeting cards and needed to replenish her supply.

She crossed the second level exit of Bloomingdale's that emptied onto the mall floor. It was four days before Christmas but she knew the Hallmark store was always fully stocked with cards, after all, greeting cards was their business.

As she moved into the mall, she walked to the right, dodging an onslaught of rushing consumers on their parade into Bloomie's. She pressed herself close to the wall as she passed by the window of Brentano's Bookstore. She glanced in and something caught her eye. She stopped in her tracks. Slowly, she turned and entered the store.

She walked to the best-selling romance rack and reached for the number two book. It was entitled *Latin Rose*. The author was Randolph Everett.

Rosa opened the back cover and stared at the picture inside. There, smiling, looking comfortable and relaxed, was Everett. She smiled at the sight of him. "He did it." 'How long has it been?' she asked herself.

'Almost a year,' the little voice in her head, which she had taken to calling Rosie, responded.

She closed the book and turned it over. The paragraph printed there described the story of Sofia, a woman torn between the loyalties to her family and the man she claimed to love. The bells of familiarity began to chime within Rosa. She wondered what he had written about her. What things were true? Which things were not? Which things, if any, were products of creative license? Without a further thought, Rosa turned and marched into the checkout line. Feelings of excitement and angst crisscrossed within her as she held this book about her, a book that thousands of people, strangers, had surely read by now.

Rosa stopped at the Hallmark store as she had planned, and then made a beeline for home. Once there, she took her time preparing dinner in an effort to convince herself that she wasn't anxious to get to the book. Finally, after an hour of dabbling in the kitchen, Rosa sat on the couch and opened *Latin Rose.*

Rosa was surprised by what Everett had written. Though it was a story based on the last year of their relationship together, it wasn't at all the blatantly scathing tale of betrayal and deceit that she expected. It was a story that described a woman who had grown angry and disillusioned with the progress of her relationship, and due to family loyalties and interference, the financial and racial pressures, and the arrival of another man who looked better on paper, couldn't release the grudge and find her way back to that relationship though promise had come to light. Rosa was angered slightly by some of the liberties Everett took in the name of creativity, and also by some of the truths she didn't want anyone to know about. Still, it gave her some comfort to know that, despite how poorly she handled their breakup, Everett had tried to convey a story about her inner conflict and pain, not her actions. In the story, Sofia made the decision that she thought was best for the man she loved, and Rosa could tell that Everett hoped she had done the same. It was clear to Rosa, even after all this time, that Everett had truly loved her.

As she turned the last page, she noticed Everett left a personal addendum. Rosa became choked up as she read his words.

To my Latin Rose, if I could only go back and erase all the missteps I made with you. If I could have been open instead of evasive, I could've built the path of communication that I knew was so vitally important to our survival as one. But alas, I fear that perhaps, had I done those things, outside forces would have caused our demise much sooner. Or maybe, just maybe, we both would've had the strength to hold on. I fear we may never know.

Still, I tried. Though it hurt me to let you go, it wasn't losing my lover and companion that pained me most. You told me, on more than one occasion, that I was your best friend and I was the one person you could always depend on. Those words were like rays of light from the sun. So, Sunshine, I say to you, the thing that caused me the most pain was that, in the end, I couldn't say the same. And still, I tried.

Rosa closed the book and sat quietly. She glanced at the wall clock. It was 2:30 am. She had a sudden urge to call Everett but thought better of it. It was late and besides, 'Would Everett even want to hear from me?' she asked herself. She wasn't exactly sure.

She rose from the couch and went into her bedroom. She placed the book on her nightstand next to the jewelry box. She opened the box and stared at the silver-plated wishbone within. Even after eleven months, the wishbone was still divided. *'No more wishes in there,'* the little Rosie voice inside her head said to her. *'So tell me?'* the voice began, *'was it worth it?'*

"Was what worth it?"

'Everything. The secrets, the lies, the confusion, letting Everett go, staying with Roberto...was it worth it? Did you get what you wanted?'

"Everett seems to be doing okay," Rosa answered aloud. "Mama and the family seem happy-"

'But what about Rosa Santos? Did you get what you wanted?' the little Rosie voice repeated.

"I don't know," she answered herself honestly. "Someone had to lose, and yes, some days I feel it was me but some days, I feel like I made the best decision I could make and, maybe, no one lost. It just is what it is, you know?"

'What have you learned from all this?'

Rosa smiled. "I learned that sometimes you have to do what's best for the people we love, even if it hurts them. And sometimes, you have to grow up, make your own decisions, and do what's right for yourself, regardless of what your friends or family think."

'And did you do that?'

Rosa looked down at *Latin Rose* and smiled. "I don't know. I'm only human, you know? I'm flawed and imperfect just like everyone else. I don't always make the smartest or bravest decisions but I did the best I could. One way or another, time will tell."

Rosa closed the jewelry box, stripped off her clothes and crawled into bed. Within minutes she was drifting off into sleep. As her consciousness slipped into quiet slumber, a vision of Everett came into her mind. She smiled. Though she was half asleep, a picture of an intact wishbone came into focus. She heard Rosie's voice whisper to her softly, "You're right, girl. Time will tell."

Rosa rolled onto her side and, finally, fell fast asleep.

PLAYING DOCTOR

By
R. Daniels

1

Doctor Michael Redlake took a deep breath as he relaxed into the long operating chair in Research Lab One. His dark brown eyes, bright with anticipation and enthusiasm, shifted in the direction of his assistant, Doctor Vera Shaw, who stood at the main operations console.

"All preparations are complete," she announced in a light, cheery voice. She glanced back at Dr. Redlake, then peered across the room at the other operating chair where Doctor Rebecca Murdock sat anxiously. "Everybody ready?" Redlake nodded. Across the room, Murdock nodded as well.

Redlake raised and tilted his head slightly as to get a better view of Doctor Murdock. "Rebecca," he called to her with a smooth, caring tone. "Last chance. You don't have to do this." He smiled.

Murdock turned her head. "I know, Michael. I want to." She returned his smile.

Shaw, standing at the console, raised an eyebrow. She sensed, as she had since the first time she met Doctor Murdock two weeks ago, that there was a strong attraction between the two doctors. Although Redlake denied it vehemently, Shaw knew the attraction was there. Shaw also knew that was the reason Doctor Murdock volunteered for the experiment. Considering the fact that Murdock was a happily married woman of twelve years, what better way for her to have her cake and eat it, too? Shaw shook her head. Was that jealousy she was feeling? How could it be? After all, she had worked with Michael Redlake for the past seven years and despite the fact that he was handsome beyond comparison, she had never once desired him. Never once had she looked at him the way Rebecca Murdock looked at him now. Or had she? And what about the dream this morning? She couldn't ignore the implications of her own subconscious. Shaw shook her head again. She decided now was not the time to explore her own feelings concerning Doctor Redlake, whatever they might be. Right now, he needed her in her capacity as a Neurobiologist. He needed her to monitor what could be the next breakthrough in the world of scientific medicine. She respected Michael Redlake and his work, and she would do her best not to let him down.

Redlake turned his gaze to Shaw. "Okay, Vera. I guess that settles it. We're ready whenever you are."

Shaw smiled warmly at Redlake, and then dropped her focus to the console in front of her. She narrated every move she made. "Activating the neural scanner." She paused. "Probing," she reported. "This should only take a minute or so," she said aloud, well aware that Redlake knew exactly what procedure she would follow and how long each would take. After all, the research was spawned from his imagination.

Murdock smiled. "It tingles."

"That's a normal response to the neural decoder as it maps your synaptic pathways. It determines the best possible route through your cerebral and visual cortexes," Redlake said from his chair.

"Okay, people," Shaw interrupted softly. "You both know the drill. I need more thought and mental energy, not verbal communication."

Redlake laughed. "Sorry, Vera."

"It's okay," she responded. She adjusted a dial and began tapping another series of buttons and commands into the control pad. "Injecting the cortical sedative. 200 mgs, now."

"Only two hundred?" Murdock questioned.

"We want you to come in easy, Doctor," Shaw said. "Just a little at a time." Shaw adjusted another dial then looked up toward Redlake.

"How do you feel, Doctor?"

"Feel?" He paused as the slightly stronger than mild sedative began to take effect. He smiled. "Nice, Vera. Real nice."

"Good," Shaw looked at the readout. "Everyone is looking good. 150 mgs more." Shaw began to smirk to herself. "I guess now would be the time to conjure up a fantasy." She looked at Redlake once again. He was, unsuccessfully, trying to stifle a small grin. Shaw knew what he was thinking as he slipped deeper into sleep. "Good luck, Doctors," she said aloud, then "Have fun," she said quietly under her breath. Shaw pressed another button, and began the procedure.

Redlake, struggling to keep his eyes open, managed one last glimpse of Doctor Murdock before he slipped into a drug-induced slumber. Although he was too tired to utter a sound, in his mind he heard her name being called by his own voice. *Rebecca.*

2

Friday, December 27, 2030.
Harvard Medical School
Boston, Massachusetts

The conference went well. Everyone present was bubbling over with excitement, anticipation, and hope for the future. Had Michael Redlake not been so tired from delivering his recent findings, he might have not been in such a hurry to get back to his hotel room to get some much needed rest before his early flight back to Annapolis in the morning. The medical conference lasted the better part of three and a half hours and, despite the fact that he was honored to have been given the chance to present his newly discovered breakthroughs, he was, without question, burning the candle at both ends.

Redlake, with his assistant and friend of seven years, Doctor Vera Shaw, arrived in Boston one day earlier to present and explain his findings that had come out of years of neural biological research. Oh, it was an exciting time. Finally, all of his theories had been proven. The profession of medical science was about to be turned on its ear due to the work of Redlake and Shaw. This breakthrough would also lend astounding benefits to the fields of psychology, psychiatry, and the criminal justice systems of the entire world. From the time they arrived, the media had surrounded Redlake. Writers from every magazine, newspaper and medical journal from every part of the globe were on hand. His every step was dogged by the unending need for the rest of the population to be in the know. Even now, after the conference was said and done, Redlake and Shaw spent another hour talking to the media and anyone else who wanted a piece of the greatest medical breakthrough since the eradication of the AIDS virus in 2025. Finally, after a draining sixty-three minutes, security broke through and escorted the two scientists safely through the crowd.

At the hotel, Vera said her goodbyes. Her son was flying in from France and she had to be at Ronald Reagan Airport in five hours to meet him, so she refused to afford herself the luxury of a quick nap beforehand. She kissed Michael affectionately on the cheek. "Get some rest, Michael," she advised. "This is only the beginning."

"Don't I know it?" he returned. "Tell Rico I said hello."

"I will," she said as she turned to go. "See you back at the lab tomorrow."

Michael watched her leave, admiring her from behind. Vera was a tall woman. She stood at approximately six feet and had a medium build. She was a *healthy woman,* as Michael liked to call her. Not too skinny, but not fat by any stretch of the imagination. She had short brown hair with a few streaks of gray that cradled her face and the back of her neck. Her eyes were hazel and her nose was small and thin. Her lips danced beneath her nose when she spoke, and Michael always had a hard time not looking at her mouth when they conversed. Though he would never let her know, he always wondered secretly what it would be like to kiss those lips, stroke her tongue softly with his, and feel the warmth of her breath on his face. This was a fantasy he always forced himself to stop having. He felt guilty in a way. Here she was assisting him with his life's work while he was fantasizing about giving each one of her ass cheeks a quick squeeze. Vera was a good friend and a talented scientist. Ever since she lost her husband six years ago, he always thought of himself as her little brother. After all, at forty- five years old, she was eight years his senior and they had grown very close, almost protective of one another. Still, he couldn't deny, big sister or not, Vera Shaw was an attractive woman. As she left, he couldn't help but notice how well her blazer, with matching skirt and accessories graced her body and swayed with her every step. Michael was sure that Vera had no idea how attractive she truly was. 'Of course,' he thought as he turned and headed for the elevator, 'the truly beautiful ones never do.'

Michael stepped into the elevator and pressed four. He waited patiently as the doors began to slide shut. A raspy female voice said, "Hold the door, please." Michael pressed the 'open' button quickly and the doors retreated into the walls. He stepped back as the woman walked into the elevator. In an instant, Michael's breath was taken away.

The woman stood at approximately five feet, eight inches tall, about two inches shorter that Michael himself. Her hair was pure blonde, so blonde, in fact, one could almost mistake it for being white. She brushed her hair every morning causing it to sit like a mane on her head and flow like a warm blanket down to the middle of her back. One stray strand of hair dangled in front of her face. As she turned toward Michael, she pushed it away from her eyes, which were a dazzling shade of green. Her cheekbones rose high on her face and her jaw was small but rounded beautifully beneath her soft pink lips. Her nose, also rounded, sat perfectly straight on her face. She smiled. Her teeth were flawless, sparkling white. She wore a blue cashmere business suit, dark blue panty hose, and plain, navy blue three-inch heels. Michael surmised that she was considerably shorter than he without the heels, while also deciding that she was, by far, the most beautiful woman he had ever seen. A surge of adrenaline ran through him as she extended her hand. A look of recognition embraced her face, then she spoke.

"Doctor Redlake." His name never sounded as good as it did when this woman said it. How he loved the thick, huskiness of her voice. "I was at the medical conference. I'm Doctor Rebecca Murdock."

The elevator doors closed.

Michael felt a surge of blood rush suddenly to his loins. He couldn't believe it. She was breathtaking, and she was a doctor, too. What more could a guy ask for? He was so completely captivated by her that he almost forgot to accept her extended greeting. As he reached for her hand, she said, "Excuse my left." She was carrying a large folder in her right hand.

"It's okay," he said as he took her hand in his. 'Yes,' he thought to himself, 'a nice, firm grip as well.' The blood pushed into his penis and his erection began to grow with every beat of his heart. The entire experience would have been perfect had his hand not felt the thin piece of soft metal that adorned her fourth finger. He looked at her hand and his heart sank slightly. There, on the finger between the middle and the pinky, sat a shiny gold band, decorated with a large diamond that threatened to harness and reflect all of the light in the elevator. He looked into her eyes, hoping she hadn't read into his disappointment at the fact that she had already exchanged nuptials with some other, very lucky, unseen bastard. Still, despite his realization, looking at her lovely face caused him to smile uncontrollably like a foolish child.

"I've been following your work for quite some time now," she said. "It's an honor to finally meet you." He released her hand.

"Thank you," he managed. 'The honor is all mine', he thought to himself. 'All mine, indeed.'

The elevator began its ascent to the fourth floor.

'Oh-my-God,' Rebecca thought to herself. She chuckled. 'This man is so fuckin' hot. I've seen him before at several medical conferences and tons of seminars, but I've never been this close to him.'

She found herself searching for something else to say, but came up with nothing. All she could do was look into the prettiest pair of dark brown eyes she had ever seen.

Michael Redlake, who was clearly of Native-American descent, stood at approximately five feet, ten inches tall. His dark, shiny, ebony hair was a beautiful complement to his caramel skin. His jaw was firm and prominent as it sloped under and supported his elevated cheekbones. His smile was wide and childlike, and his teeth were flawless. His build was that of a man who took time to frequent the gym on a regular basis, which she found amazing given the amount of time he must devote to his career. He was adorned in a casual two-piece, tan colored suit. His crisp, white Pierre Cardin shirt sat beautifully under the tan paisley tie that hung from his neck. 'Goddamn, he's beautiful.' Rebecca thought of her colleague back in D.C., Doctor Brittany Sutton. 'Wait until I tell, Brit. She's going to die.'

Michael broke the silence. "So, you're...um, a doctor? What-uh-?"

"I'm a psychiatrist," she said.

"A psychiatrist?" he repeated for lack of other words.

Rebecca felt like a schoolgirl looking into the face of her first crush. "Yeah, nothing as illustrious as a neurobiologist, of course."

He grinned. He spoke slowly. He didn't want to stumble over his words. "Hey, don't sell psychiatry short. The world needs you just as much as it needs me."

She stifled a giggle. She glanced at the elevator control pad nervously. He followed her gaze, then asked quickly, "I'm sorry, what floor?"

Rebecca looked at the panel. The number four had been illuminated. She felt a pang of guilt when she realized suddenly that she wanted to go to the fourth floor, too. She was a married woman, happily married. Joseph was a wonderful husband and they shared an exciting and joyous life together. Although she had no intention of betraying her husband over some man who had always served as a distant, private fantasy, she couldn't deny the overwhelming attraction she had for him. Not just the physical attraction, but years of admiring his work, his ideas, his determination against other prominent scientists in his field who doubted his imagination and his vision. The attraction ran so much deeper than flesh. It touched her on several levels- mental, intellectual, and oh yes, she had to admit, sexual. "Seven," she said finally. Michael pushed the number seven and it lit up under his finger. Even as he did, the elevator slowed as it approached the fourth floor.

"Where do you practice?" he asked quickly, trying to fit as much conversation as he could into the short, few seconds he had left.

She smiled. Her smile was gorgeous. She took a small, clearly unintentional step towards him. "D.C.," she said, resisting the urge to say 'not far from Annapolis.' She didn't want him to know that she had been secretly infatuated with him for years and knew exactly where he worked. Then again, in the medical world, he was a well-known, respected figure. That fact that he worked at Silverleaf was probably common knowledge.

The door opened to the fourth floor.

For the first time since she stepped into the elevator, Michael sensed that her interest in him might not be purely professional. God, how that turned him on even more. His hard-on began to pulse beneath his wool pants. As much as he didn't want to leave her presence, he didn't want to risk her noticing the ever-growing bulge in his slacks. Before stepping forward, he shifted his weight slightly from side to side in an inconspicuous effort to jockey his hard-on into a more comfortable position. He crossed the elevator's threshold onto the fourth floor. He turned to her slightly, in an effort to conceal his blood-filled cock. "That's great. I work at Silverleaf in Annapolis."

She reached and pressed the 'open' button to keep the door from closing before she was ready. *'Rebbie, what are you doing?'* she asked herself. He noticed her nervousness. He laughed.

"If you're ever in the area, maybe we can do lunch," he suggested. He wanted to say dinner but the implications of dinner are all too often connected with candlelight, a romantic atmosphere, intimately playful conversation, and whatever else that followed. Lunch seemed more like an innocent-middle of the day-in plain view type of offer. Even though she was married, he didn't want to scare her off.

"Sounds good," she replied. "I'd love to hear more about Mental Imaging." She tried to make it sound as if she just wanted to meet him to discuss his work, two doctors having a platonic meeting of the minds, so to speak. The problem was, the only person she was trying to convince of that fact was herself. She let go of the button.

"Great," he said. "You know where to find me." *'Damn. I hope I didn't sound too eager.'*

The doors began to close.

"See ya later," she managed to say before the doors closed between them. 'Lunch,' she laughed to herself. 'I *never* eat lunch.'

3

Monday, December 30, 2030.
The practice of Sutton, Murdock, &
Crow, Ph.d's.
Washington D.C.

Brittany Sutton walked into Rebecca Murdock's private office and closed the door behind herself. Rebecca's last patient of the day had just left and now Rebecca was free for the rest of the afternoon. Brittany was a pleasingly plain looking woman of forty years. Not plain in the sense that she appeared unattractive or boring. Plain in the sense that she didn't go out of her way to draw attention to herself when it came to her personal appearance. Her skin was smooth and as dark as cocoa. Her hair was tied back into a bun and a pair of black-framed reading glasses dangled on a chain around her neck. She was a petite woman who stood at five feet six inches tall. She adorned herself in the finest business attire that she could afford and never had a hair out of place. Brittany despised wearing heavy perfumes and feminine colognes. She preferred the scents of light body oils and soft natural fragrances such as Hawaiian Flower, Kiwi Rose, and Focus. When it came to cosmetic enhancements such as makeup, Brittany took the minimalist route. Her skin was so soft and vibrant that she had no need for foundations or powders. She added just a hint of soft red to her lips and wore no eye makeup of any kind. She refused to color her nails, except for the weekly upkeep of a clear French manicure. She was indeed, a natural beauty.

She walked to Rebecca's desk and took the seat on the other side. She looked at Rebecca, who had her feet on the desk and was grinning from ear to ear. Brittany sat quietly and stared at her long time colleague and friend for what seemed like forever. Finally, when she could stand the silence no longer, she burst into laughter. "Girl, if you don't give me the details right now, I'm going to have to hurt you. I've been waiting all day for this."

Rebecca whispered, "Oh, Brit. It's terrible. I feel so guilty."

"Guilty? Why? You didn't do anything."

"I know, but I wish I had," she laughed, trying to keep her voice down. "That's what I feel guilty about."

Brittany leaned onto Rebecca's desk, arms folded beneath her. "You shouldn't. Just because you're married doesn't mean you aren't entitled to your own fantasies. And stop whispering, I sent the secretary home and ol' Howard left for the day."

Rebecca sighed heavily. "Fantasies?" she said, her raspy voice back at normal levels. "I practically told the guy I'd have lunch with him. There's got to be something wrong in that alone."

"Why?"

"Because it's something that I could never tell Joseph, that's why." Rebecca rose from her chair and sat on the edge of her desk. "Joseph adores me, Brit. He's so good to me."

"For goodness sake, Rebbie. You didn't fuck the guy." Rebecca turned her head slowly towards Brittany but said nothing. A smirk caressed her lips. Brittany smiled. "But you wanted to. Didn't you?"

Rebecca leapt off the edge of the desk as if the surface were hot. "Oh, man. You don't understand, Brit. We've seen so many pictures of this guy, this hot, young doctor, who seemed too good to be true. Then I run into him in the elevator, and, oh...he's gorgeous. God, Brit, you should've come."

"Believe me, I did plenty of that," she said with a smile.

"Oh, that's right. How is Mister Tall, Dark and Hung like a Horse?"

Brittany laughed, "Oh, God. Les would die if he knew I told you that."

"Hell, girl, what else is there to tell?"

Brittany opened her mouth as if she planned to respond but said nothing.

"Exactly," Rebecca chuckled. They raised their hands in unison and imitated the sound of a train whistle as it blows into a station on a cool fall morning. "Really, though. I have no intention of calling the guy, but I thought about him all weekend."

Brittany narrowed her gaze playfully. "Did he play mental substitute?"

"What?" Rebecca asked. "No way. I love Joseph. I wouldn't dream of fantasizing about another man while we were making love."

"I didn't say you don't love Joseph. That wasn't the question. Nor did I ask you what you would dream of doing. The question was-"

"I know what the question was," she interrupted. Silence. Then she burst into laughter.

"I knew it," Brittany said.

"Brit, I'll never admit it with these lips. Do you hear me?"

Brittany laughed. "It's okay. I hear you, girl. But I'll tell you one thing. Don't let me run into him, because I won't hesitate to counsel him personally."

"You're not married though."

Brittany smiled. "Thank God for that."

Monday, December 30, 2030.
The home of Doctor Michael Redlake
Annapolis, Maryland

Michael paced around the apartment as he looked into the screen of the viewphone. Vera Shaw was on the other line discussing with him the particulars of the first phase of experiments on the Mental Imaging Project. Shaw insisted that they wait until the end of the week before inserting a human subject into the project. But Michael wanted to push ahead of schedule and take the first steps as soon as possible.

"Tomorrow morning sounds good to me, Vera!" He knew she would object as soon as he said it.

"Michael, you know it would take at least two days to round up the rest of the team. We need the entire staff present in order to insure that all of the safety protocols are being observed and monitored closely, at least until all of the autonomic systems are installed." Vera sighed heavily and raised an eyebrow. Michael knew she was right. Vera knew that he knew she was right. She continued. "I know that you're anxious to get this project moving and I don't blame you. So am I. But the last thing we need right now is to rush into it and possibly endanger someone's life."

Michael conceded. "You're right! I guess all the excitement over this past weekend has me ready to go. I don't know what I was thinking." He was lying. He knew exactly what he was thinking. Ever since he met Doctor Rebecca Murdock, all he could think about was seeing her again. Her face was etched permanently into his thoughts and as long as he could picture her face accurately, the Mental Imaging Probe would do the rest. Of course, he hadn't even mentioned to Vera that he had met someone, let alone a married someone. He knew that Vera wouldn't approve. Not to mention, he also hadn't lobbied the idea to Vera of him becoming the first subject of his own work. He knew she was going to have definite reservations about that.

"Get some rest, Michael. You looked pretty wiped out at work today and you still sound exhausted," she said in a nurturing tone. "We can discuss this at work tomorrow. Okay?"

He smiled. "Yes, Doctor." They exchanged goodbyes and Michael tapped a button and severed the visual link to Vera's viewphone. He stood silently and stared at the blank screen. Already he was thinking of the many avenues around the argument Vera would present once he told her of his wishes to be the first guinea pig. He chuckled to himself. *'Maybe if I slipped a tongue in her, she'd come around,'* he thought and then laughed aloud. He began to step away from the screen but then stopped. "Computer," he called, "display phone book entry RM1." Instantly, the phone number and address of Sutton, Murdock and Crow appeared on the screen. The words *Ready to Dial* were flashing in bright blue letters. He hesitated. Since he had located her work number on the Bell Atlantic Interface Directory, he pulled up her number every day. But he couldn't bring himself to call. She was married for Christ sake, what did he honestly expect from her? He nibbled on his lower lip. "Cancel." The screen went blank. He was sure he would pull her number again tomorrow. Maybe then he would have the nerve to call her. Maybe. Maybe not.

Wednesday, January 15, 2031.
Silverleaf Eatery and Commons
Annapolis, Maryland

Michael smiled across the table at Rebecca. He couldn't believe she was here. She was absolutely beautiful. After the seminar today, Michael had planned to go home and get some sleep. With all of the time consuming work that he, Vera and the rest of the team had done over the last two weeks on Phase One, he needed some rest. He reported the success of Phase One today at the seminar. Just two days ago, Michael became the first subject of his own experiment, and the green light for Phase Two was flashing brightly. He hadn't even made it off the platform before he heard a familiar voice calling his name. He turned, and there she was, looking just as stunning and radiant as she did the first time he laid eyes on her. He led her to his favorite eatery on the other side of the Silverleaf district where they ate soy based beef stew, watercress sandwiches, and sipped on spring water.

"So, explain Phase Two to me," she said in a husky tone.

"It's simple, really." He grinned, feeling embarrassed suddenly. "It's an extension of Phase One. Instead of tapping into the mental images of one subject, we tap into two separate subjects and integrate their..." he paused, "fantasies or whatever images happen to be conjured up."

Her eyes lit up. "That's incredible. Do you plan on undergoing the experiment again?"

"No," he answered. "I'd like to be on the outside this time. I figured

I would give someone else a chance to experience it. Why? Are you interested?" he joked, assuming she would decline.

She countered his question with another question. "Were you able to control your imagery output while the experiment was going on or does it pull images randomly from your cerebral cortex?"

"Control it? You mean, initiate the image produced on the screen and dictate its course? Yes, somewhat. Once you've chosen a course, if the mind tends to wander, sometimes the conjured event can snowball into something else."

Her eyes narrowed and her cheeks rose slightly. "Sort of like a runaway fantasy?"

He tried to conceal his smile, unsuccessfully. "Yes, sort of. Yes."

"Then, yes," she said.

"Yes?"

"I'm interested."

Michael remained silent as he searched her face for any sign that she may be joking. He found none. "You do realize that someone will be monitoring the images? They will see every picture your mind produces."

"I realize that, Michael."

His heart jumped. That was the first time she had addressed him as Michael. Up until now they had only addressed each other with strict formality. "Yes, but, your fantasies will be somewhat guided, or influenced by the other person involved. If the other person conjures up unwanted images, you could develop feelings of invasion. If that happens, who knows what that could manifest into?"

Rebecca sat back in her chair and raised her chin slightly. "Michael, I'm going to be honest with you, okay? I'm sure it was abundantly obvious that I was attracted to you in the elevator in Boston, and I'd be lying if I said that I haven't thought about you every day since. But, as circumstances would have it, I am a married woman. Happily married, in fact. Joseph is a wonderful man and I would never do anything to hurt him."

Michael, although he respected her last statement, was disappointed.

"I wouldn't ask you to."

"Thank you," she said. She smiled shyly. "However, I don't like to deny what's inside me." She leaned closer to him. "How accurate is the sensory perception for the subject of the experiment?"

"One hundred percent. The Imaging Inducer reroutes images directly from your synaptic pathways through your cerebral and visual cortexes, the cerebral nerve centers, along the Central Nervous System, memory centers and motor receptors. The mind perceives the feedback stimuli from the fantasy as real. The subject feels everything. Pain from the fantasy is felt as pain. Pleasure is felt as pleasure. It sounds scary, I know."

"Not at all. In fact," she hesitated. "I want you, Michael. I know it sounds like some adolescent desire, considering I hardly know you, but I do. The only reason I didn't contact you was because I am married. But when I heard that you were trying to integrate the fantasies of two separate subjects, well...I just decided that I might be able to have my cake and eat it, too. I'd love to be your subject for Phase Two, Michael, but I would love it more if you were in there with me."

"You could have me without actually having me," he said.

Rebecca smiled. "Anything in the name of scientific research."

Michael's eyes shifted behind Rebecca. In the distance, Vera Shaw approached the table. He and Vera came here for lunch quite often over the past few years. "There you are," she said as she stepped within earshot. Michael began to rise from his chair but Vera waved him back down. She rounded the table and although she was speaking to Michael, her eyes were drawn inadvertently to the very attractive blonde sitting opposite him. "I thought I might find you here."

Rebecca extended her hand immediately. "Doctor Shaw, it's an honor to finally meet you. I've followed your and Doctor Redlake's research for years."

Taking the woman's hand in her own and giving it a firm shake, Vera replied, "Thank you. What a nice thing to say, Miss...?" Vera guarded her demeanor. Why was she feeling defensive all of a sudden?

"Doctor Rebecca Murdock," she said with a smile. "And it's Mrs., actually."

"Doctor?" Vera asked, ignoring the reference that Rebecca was married.

"I'm a psychiatrist."

Vera's expression relaxed slightly. "Analyzing the good Doctor Redlake here?"

"Who says I need analyzing?" Michael chimed in.

"Who says you don't?" Vera retorted quickly.

"He's a pretty open and shut study, Doctor Shaw. I had him all figured out when we met in Boston last month," she laughed. "There's no mystery there."

"Boston? At the conference?" Vera looked at Michael. He made no mention of meeting a woman in Boston. Not that he had to report every woman he meets, it's just that, well, he always did. Why did he not mention this one? Michael appeared to be slightly uncomfortable. He was attracted to this woman. She had no doubts about that. Vera returned her gaze to Rebecca. Her cheeks had reddened slightly. Vera sensed that Rebecca's reference to Boston was a slip up. She knew that there was more going on here than a platonic lunch. She realized suddenly why Rebecca made it a point to tell her that she was married. She smiled at Rebecca, "He's been so tired from that damn conference he didn't even mention it." Vera took a step backwards as if she was trying to leave. Rebecca spoke up to stop her.

"Won't you join us?"

"No, I need to get back-"

"Please," Rebecca looked into Vera's eyes. "I need another woman at the table to keep me from ordering dessert. You understand, guilty pleasures and all that."

Vera did understand. Although this woman clearly had feelings for Michael, Vera knew that she had reservations about being left alone with opportunity to act upon them. Vera decided that she respected that. She smiled, pulled out a chair and sat down. "Thank you, Doctor Murdock. How kind of you." Vera looked at Michael. He was clearly uncomfortable with this situation. Vera smiled at him, and then turned to Rebecca. "So, tell me all about the world of psychiatry. Where do you practice?"

Rebecca stole a quick glance at Michael before turning to Vera. She knew that she had gotten her point across to him before Vera showed up. Now it was just a matter of time before he would call her and set her wishes into motion.

4

Vera struggled. She was caught in a dream that frightened her. She tossed and turned in an effort to wake herself, but to no avail. Her subconscious had her in a wrench-like grip that promised no immediate release from the prison of her own denied fantasies.

Deep in her mind, she found herself in the lab. She was clad in the navy blue flannel pajamas that she wore to bed every single night. Her white lab coat hung open over her nightclothes. Her feet were cold. She glanced down and discovered herself to be barefoot. She glanced up at the lab door. Instinctively, she ran towards it and lunged at the handle. Locked. "Shit," she cursed. Suddenly, there was a soft rustling behind her. Vera froze. She closed her eyes but did not turn. Tears began to stream from behind her shut eyelids as the rustling sound continued. She took a deep breath, opened her eyes, and began to turn around slowly. There, across the room, lying on the lab table were Doctor Redlake and Doctor Murdock. Both were naked, covered only by a white sheet. They were wrapped in each other's arms.

Despite her conscious desire to hold her position, she found herself walking slowly towards the table. With each step, the moans of pleasure became more audible. The smell of sex became more pungent. Vera stopped at the tableside. The two doctors were seemingly unaware of her presence. She wanted to take a step back. She even ordered her feet to do so. Nothing. Not one single movement. Her body was fixed to the spot. Her eyes were glued to the two gyrating, naked, sweaty bodies on the table.

Vera took a breath and located her voice. "Stop," she said softly. They didn't respond. They didn't even look up. "Stop!" she said slightly louder. Doctor Redlake rolled on top of Doctor Murdock. The sheet slipped off his back and fell silently to the floor. In response, Doctor Murdock positioned herself under the handsome doctor. She spread her legs and reached for his manhood with her left hand. Vera gasped for she felt the heat of Redlake's pulsating penis in *her* left hand. She shook her hand but couldn't shake the feeling of having a hot, throbbing penis in her grasp. On the table, Redlake lowered his head and kissed Murdock on the neck. Again, Vera experienced the sensation. She felt the warmth of his kiss, the wetness of his tongue, and the hot flow of air from his breath. The sensation sent a tepid gush of moistness straight to her loins. Murdock pulled his member closer to her waiting flesh. "No," managed to escape from Vera's lips. Closer. "No, please," Vera pleaded softly. Murdock lifted her hips as Redlake thrust violently downward into her. Vera, standing at the tableside, stiffened. Her head fell back as she fought to contain the sensation of having his hot shaft embedded deep within her. She tried to stifle a scream but could not. Her mouth opened and a howl of pleasure echoed from her throat. She felt an orgasm building within her. Her insides tightened. On the table, Murdock exclaimed through bated breath, "Oh, God, here I come". Vera lost her breath as the shared climax began to overtake her and shake her from within. Then, without warning, she woke from her dream.

Her brow was covered in sweat, her flannel pajamas damp from the same. She was breathing heavily. Her body still shook from the orgasm that ripped through her body as she slept. She wiped her forehead. Then, she ran her left hand down her body, past her breast, to the hot crevice between her legs. She closed her eyes as she reached inside her pajamas and her fingers slid into the pool of wetness between her thighs. Quietly, she lay there. It was almost ten minutes before she was calm enough to look at the clock and realize what time it was. 5:02

a.m. Time to get up. Today was the day. Today was the day Phase Two began.

Sunday, January 26, 2031.
Silverleaf Research Facility
Annapolis, Maryland

Vera glanced into the CSP (Cerebral Synaptic Perceptual) Monitor. Despite the fact that she was well aware of what she expected to see as the images began to form, as a scientist, it would still be a fascinating experience. A first in medical science.

She peered closer as the first electronic spark shot across the monitor, then another, then another. The sparks began to fill the screen rapidly and move in what seemed, at first, to be a random dance of illuminated particles. Then suddenly, the sparks began to gravitate to each other in set intervals about three seconds apart. Vera expected this. She nodded. *So far, so good.* She raised her head and looked at Michael in the chair. His expression was one of peace, comfort, and contentment. She smiled and turned her attention to Rebecca in the opposite chair. Her expression was as calm and peaceful as Michael's. Vera checked the autonomic systems relay. Every ounce of data was flowing onto her display. From where she stood, she could monitor the entire procedure.

The CSP sensor emitted a quick beep. Vera glanced at the monitor. It was starting. It was only a matter of minutes now before she would know whether Phase Two of Michael Redlake's brainchild project was a success. An image began to take shape on the monitor. Vera, focusing on the screen, stood transfixed as the images began to form and mesh. She adjusted a dial slowly. As she did, the distortion on the screen began to clear. She tapped a button. The lines gained definition and the images became sharper. Vera gasped as the first recognizable image graced the monitor in front of her. She raised her hand to her mouth, but despite her initial instinct to look away, her eyes remained fixed.

She watched attentively as the image formed on the screen in front of her. From a scientific point of view, it was amazing. From a personal point of view, it was terrifying. There on the monitor was the merging of two separate fantasy images into one. Two separate and distinct mental pictures being influenced and guided by the other to form one coherent fantasy. There, almost exactly as Vera Shaw had dreamed earlier, lay Doctor Redlake and Doctor Murdock. Naked, intertwined, and lost in passion.

Vera checked the autonomic systems relays. Everything was going well. So far, this experiment was a success. Now the only thing to do was to sit back and let the two fantasies merge and coexist as one.

Phase Two

The floor and the walls in the room were white. Each wall was adorned with two large bay windows that allowed streams of sunlight to flood into the room and wash over the grand, king-sized, brass bed located in the center. The sheets on the bed were white as well. The room was spacious, and for all intents and purposes, immaculate. It contained an air of purity and comfort only found in the fleeting fantasies of dreamers and lovers. Fortunately, in this case, it was nothing less than perfect. The room was completely quiet, save the unmistakable sounds of passionate, uninhibited sex.

Michael's tan body rested comfortably on Rebecca's white flesh. Their tongues lashed out and fought to control the other's mouth. Their bodies moved together as if they were choreographed into the perfect sexual dance. Their legs continually wrapped and unwrapped themselves around the other's. Their hands grabbed and pulled at the other's body, trying to bring them even closer than physically possible.

Michael disengaged the wet kiss and began to move his kisses down Rebecca's torso. He licked at her hot flesh, which sent sharp pricks of pleasure through her body. He cupped her right breast in his hand and tongued the nipple softly. He began working the entire nipple into his mouth. Being certain not to neglect any part of her body, his other hand was busy massaging her other breast, preparing it for the inevitable tongue he was to bring to it in a matter of seconds.

Waves of hot pleasure careened through her body. Rebecca reached down and grabbed at Michael's throbbing member. It pulsed in her grasp and she tightened her grip slightly. She began stroking it, up and down, up and down. Soon, she could hear that his breathing had fallen into sync with each stroke of his now hungry penis. It was not long before Rebecca began to lose control.

Suddenly, she pushed at his shoulders and forced him onto his back. Realizing he had to relinquish control of her breasts, Michael complied reluctantly. She moved down his body and positioned her head between his legs. She took his penis in her hand and continued to stroke it. She lowered her head and began to caress his balls lightly with her tongue. Michael jerked as her soft, wet tongue stroked his nuts and her hot breath blanketed his scrotum with warmth. She continued to pump his cock with her hand as she ran her tongue back and forth along his sensitive testicles. With each lashing of her tongue, Michael released a moan of pleasure and approval. Slowly, with her hand still jerking him, she moved her tongue down further until she reached the spot just beneath his balls. That oh-so-sensitive spot. There, she focused all of her tongue's efforts and begin licking at his flesh. In response, Michael's legs began to shake uncontrollably. Rebecca quickened the pace on his penis and applied a little more pressure with her tongue. "Oh God," Michael exclaimed as Rebecca licked and stroked him endlessly. Her tongue began to move up and down, back and forth between his swollen balls and the most sensitive spot on his body. His breathing increased and his pelvis began to gyrate. Suddenly, Rebecca ran her tongue up his balls and onto his shaft. She kissed the base of his penis and moved her free hand to his balls. Slowly, she kissed her way to the head of his pulsating cock, opened her mouth and took him in.

Michael's body tensed slightly. Rebecca placed her right hand at the base of his cock, while her left caressed his balls. With his member firmly in place, she moved up and down his cock with long, even strokes.

She held his cock gently, allowing the sides of her mouth to envelope it in complete warmth as she sucked on it. Rebecca massaged his balls as her tongue licked at his member from all sides. Gradually, she increased the pace, but didn't stray from her avenue of technique. She sucked in long, even, quick strokes. Michael jerked beneath her as she took the length of his cock into her hot mouth again and again. Michael's breathing became louder and he began to groan with every rise and fall of her mouth on him. Rebecca felt his cock stiffen suddenly in her mouth. The head of his penis swelled at the back of her throat. She knew he was at the edge of an earth-shaking orgasm. She squeezed his balls lightly and continued to suck on him. "Oh God," he exclaimed again. His body jerked and his penis twitched as it filled beyond capacity with his come. Rebecca took in his penis down to the base. Michael could hold back no longer. He moaned loudly and released his load into her awaiting mouth. Rebecca gulped at his hot, salty jism like she had never done before. In reality, Rebecca had never swallowed in her life. Oh, she had tried many times for her husband, but due to an uncontrollable gag reflex, she could never do it. But here, in the realm of fantasy, anything was possible. Feeling his hot come in her mouth sent several hot flashes straight to her, now, dripping pussy. She knew it wouldn't be long before she would have to have a hot cock buried deep inside her.

Finally, Michael's orgasm subsided. Rebecca held his penis in her mouth and caressed it softly with her tongue. As his breathing returned to normal, she began to move her mouth up and down again, this time, ever so gently. This continued for several minutes before Michael lifted his head and began maneuvering Rebecca's body around into the Sixty-nine position above him. He pulled at her and she began to lower her wetness towards his mouth. With an expected jerk, he pulled her dripping pussy onto his face and extended his tongue as far as it would reach inside her. Rebecca released a moan of pleasure that filled the empty room with a passionate echo.

Michael extended his tongue and licked feverishly at her labia. Rebecca began to move in rhythm with his probing tongue. Michael reached up and pulled the weight of her body down onto his face, encouraging her to grind all her pleasures into him. She complied easily.

Michael pulled his extended tongue back slightly so that he could lick at the opening of her pussy as she pushed into his face. Several bolts of pleasure interrupted her gyrations as he sucked and licked her female essence. She began to jerk uncontrollably. He grabbed at her to hold her in place. Pools of female dew poured down his face as he, once again, attempted to lick deeper and deeper inside of her. She ground her clitoris into his mouth, which in turn caused her pubic bone to rub against his chin with every stroke. Pleasure shot through her body. She threw her head back, her body now in an upright position, and she reached for the brass railings at the foot of the bed for leverage. She was gyrating uncontrollably now. Michael's tongue moved in perfect tandem with her body. Then, she felt it begin.

Her insides began to tighten like a rope being twisted upon itself. Tighter and tighter it became as the ensuing orgasm began to build towards its climactic peak. Rebecca screamed in pleasure and her gyrations became shorter as she fought to keep the pressure in one place. Michael held her even tighter as she ground her aching, wet pussy into his face. Not wanting her to lose it, he kept his tongue motions constant. The knot inside her tightened even more and would soon become so constricted that it would eventually snap. Michael's tongue lashed forward into her G-spot. Rebecca jerked. Her head fell back and she closed her eyes. Her mouth opened to release a scream but nothing came out. Still, she continued to grind his face beneath her. Then, it happened. The knot inside her gave way, snapping with such a force that she had to fight to stay mounted on Michael's tongue. Hot waves of pleasure were sent into each part of her body like ripples being sent out from a dropped pebble in a pool of water. A scream of pleasure managed to escape her open mouth as every appendage felt the release of tension inside her. Every inch of her body shivered, then relaxed.

Michael wasted no time. He lifted himself up, rolled Rebecca onto her back and pushed his cock deep into her. Rebecca wrapped her legs around his back and locked him in. They began to move in unison, grinding gently at first, but then pumping at a gradually accelerating pace. As the pace continued to quicken, Michael and Rebecca breathed louder and heavier. They fought to keep the momentum going as their bodies began to sweat and their desires moved from sexual passion to primitive sexual abandonment. Their kisses became harder and longer, their tongues probed deeper into each other's mouths and their every action intensified.

Rebecca pushed him off of her suddenly. She turned herself over on all fours and lowered her head on the pillow. Michael didn't hesitate. He pulled her closer to him and parted her pussy lips from behind. With only the head of the penis inside her, he began to pump slowly. Rebecca was having no part of that. She backed onto his penis violently, taking in all of him. She continued to slide back and forth feverishly until Michael got the message and picked up the pace on his own. Uncontrollably, Michael slammed into her from behind over and over. Rebecca howled with pleasure as Michael's cock pushed into her again and again. "Oh… God….don't…stop…" she managed to say between his forceful thrusts. For what seemed like hours, they crashed into each other. Harder and harder they pumped, closer and closer they became.

They both began to breath heavily; their bodies were covered in sweat. Closer and closer. The temperature in the room began to rise. Closer. Harder. The two became lost in each other. Soon, they became so close that it was hard to determine where he ended and she began. They continued to pump. Harder. Closer. They both began to approach their climax, but this time something was different. Something was different about the way they felt now. Despite this feeling, they continued to move into one another as if they were compelled to move closer and closer into each other's bodies. Their climaxes peaked and they both screamed out in indescribable bliss. Michael continued to thrust deeply into her. Rebecca met every stroke with a counterstroke of her own. Her body shook with an intense orgasm as Michael's cock spat jism deep inside of her. Then, something happened.

Michael pushed his pulsating member into her and his entire midsection morphed and disappeared inside her body. Rebecca moaned and opened her legs even wider. Michael continued to gyrate and thrust into her, each time their bodies merged deeper and deeper into one entity. Instinctively, both of them knew that something was wrong. Despite the pleasure, something wasn't quite right. Still, they couldn't stop. They were caught in a fantasy that had escaped from both of them. Despite their desire to stop, their inner desire and uncontained primal lust for each other kept them trapped. Michael tried to concentrate. He tried to focus on the experiment itself, but he couldn't. Whenever his mind would wander, his desire for Rebecca would pull him further into the dream. Whenever Rebecca tried to pull herself free, her yearning for him would tighten the grip. Slowly, their senses became overloaded and reached the point where pleasure became pain. Everything in the room began to dull from white to gray. Rebecca screamed. Michael felt her pain and screamed as well. Still thrusting and still merging, they both began to come again. Only this time, the pleasure was too intense, too overwhelming. Their bodies crashed into each other's and they merged completely. Then, everything went black.

Sunday, January 26, 2031.
Silverleaf Research Facility
Annapolis, Maryland

It took only fifteen minutes before Doctor Redlake and Doctor Murdock were out of the Mental Imager and the machine could be powered down. Vera tapped the controls and the power level began to drop. She looked at the two doctors as they became fully coherent again and aware of being back in the real world. Although they hadn't gone anywhere physically, Vera noted that they both were perspiring heavily and were extremely fatigued. '*Spent* would be a better word,' she thought to herself. Spent with good reason. Vera saw the entire fantasy as it happened.

Michael called to her. "What happened? Did everything go...all right?"

Vera smiled at Michael as she crossed the room to disconnect him from the Synaptic Probe. She looked him in the eyes. "Everything was fine. The project was a success. But I had to pull you out at the end."

"Had to? Why?"

"You don't remember?" she asked him.

"I remember making love. It was so intense, so vivid. Then it just stopped. Did something go wrong?"

"The Neural Decoder had a little trouble keeping up with all the sensory information. Nothing to worry about," she assured him. "The fantasies began to cascade towards the end."

"What do you mean exactly?" Rebecca called from across the room.

"Your bodies began to merge."

"What?" Rebecca exclaimed. "That's imp-". Rebecca stopped.

Vera released Michael. "How do you feel?" He took a deep breath and nodded. Vera turned and headed for Rebecca. She began disconnecting her from the Probe. She looked at Rebecca and smiled. "How do you feel?"

"I'm fine," she said. She touched Vera's arm. Their eyes met. "Nothing is impossible in the world of fantasy, is it?"

"I'm afraid not. Luckily I pulled you out as the cascade began. We can review the logs of your brain patterns at the onset of the cascade whenever you two are up to it. I'd also like to give you both a thorough examination. As of yet, we have no way of knowing how a cascade affects the actual physical body."

"Good thing you were here," Rebecca said.

Vera smiled but didn't respond. Rebecca wasn't sure if that meant Vera wasn't happy that she witnessed their fantasy or if she wished she had been a part of it. Vera walked to the controls. "Anyway. For all intents and purposes, Phase Two was a success."

Michael looked over at Rebecca and she returned his gaze. They smiled at each other. They had experienced something no other person on the planet had experienced. Yet. Michael wondered if the world was ready.

Sunday, January 26, 2031
Silverleaf Eatery and Commons
Annapolis, Maryland

Michael and Rebecca enjoyed an early dinner, discussed their future plans in their respective practices and prepared to bid each other farewell. Throughout the entire meal, neither of them mentioned the experience of the day.

After dinner, they walked across Silverleaf Field towards her car. They held hands and looked into the sky, but they spoke very little. Finally, Rebecca broke the silence. "Thank you for dinner. It was wonderful."

"My pleasure," he said as he patted his stomach. "I feel like I ate everything in the restaurant. I'm stuffed."

"We had a pretty nice sized lunch before Phase Two."

"I don't know what's gotten into me," he said. "I *never* eat lunch."

"Very funny," she laughed. "From what I've seen, you eat lunch every day."

Michael thought for a minute then realized she was right. "Yeah, I do." He chuckled at himself. "What was I thinking?"

They arrived at Rebecca's car, a black 2030 Lincoln Town Car, and Michael kissed her on the forehead. "Give me a call every once in a while," he said to her.

"Don't worry," she smiled. "I will." She reached up and touched his cheek, and for one quick instant she had a sudden urge to give each one of his ass cheeks a quick squeeze. *'Where did that come from?'* she thought. Her smile widened as she considered it, but then the urge left as quickly as it had come. She turned to Michael. "Keep up the good work, Doctor Redlake. You're an incredible man." With that, she got into her car, started the engine, and drove off. She didn't look back.

Michael watched her go, then turned and walked across the large field that led back to the Research Facility. He thought about how his work would affect the rest of the world. He thought about what new theories he would come up with in the future. But he knew, deep down, that no matter what work he followed, he would always be most proud of his Mental Imaging-Synaptic Probe theories. Not because of the recognition and the prestige it would offer him, but because of his one chance meeting with a most wonderful woman. A woman he would never forget. A woman who would find her way into his fantasies for all the days to come.

HEADS OR TAILS

By

R. Daniels

ONE

Victor leafed through Olivia's photo album as he waited for her to return from the kitchen. They had rehearsed their scene for acting class for a good portion of the evening and were now ready to set aside the script and give it a shot 'off-book'. Olivia confessed that she worked better once she had a hot cup of tea to ease her nerves. She offered Victor a cup as well and he accepted.

Victor paced back and forth in the living room as he recited silently his lines from Michael Weller's play, *Loose Ends*. He passed a small mirror mounted over a makeshift fireplace and paused to take in his image. He was a young, handsome, Japanese-American of twenty-two years. His parents were first generation immigrants to the United States and, due to the constant flow of White Sox fans, Cubs fans, Bulls fans, and Bears fans, found Chicago to be a suitable place to lay down roots and open an authentic Japanese restaurant. Victor had worked in his family's restaurant all his life but had dreamed of becoming a working actor since he was a small child. This dream led him to the Player's Workshop at the Chicago Center for Performing Arts. This is where he had been studying the craft of acting for three years. This is also where he met the girl of his dreams. Olivia Tyler. Olivia had been studying at the Center for well over a year before they were paired for *Loose Ends*. It was the happiest day of Victor's life.

The sound of the Red Line pulling into the Wrigleyville stop a few blocks away shook Victor's gaze away from the mirror. He turned towards the kitchen as Olivia emerged into the dim light that illuminated the short hallway between the two rooms. Just the sight of her made him smile. Olivia returned his smile and handed him a saucer with a hot cup of tea on top. He took the tea and watched her as she sat down and placed her tea on the coffee table in front of the sofa. He smiled again. *Oh, man. She is beautiful.*

Olivia Tyler had lived in Chicago all her life. She grew up right there in Wrigleyville and, even now, lived within a few blocks of the home where her parents still resided. She was a beautiful, African-American girl of twenty-three years. Her skin was the shade of deep mocha. Her hair, which she kept pulled back into a tight bun, was thick and shiny. Her body rivaled the physique of actress and pop star Jennifer Lopez, except Olivia had larger breasts and darker skin. Confidence and self-security oozed from every step she took and she had no problem bringing those assets to her acting. She had received a B.F.A in Acting from Northern Illinois University just eighteen months prior and continued to study at the Center for Performing Arts where she had been practicing for shortly over a year. Olivia was a brilliant actress. As far back as she could remember, acting was the only career she'd ever dreamed of and she was determined to let nothing get in her way. She enjoyed the lessons she learned and the freedom of expression that she was allowed to explore while studying at the Center. Olivia was never satisfied unless she was delivering a performance that was 'in the pocket', and nothing turned her on more than working with an actor who was as dedicated as she. That's what turned her on to Victor. On stage, Victor was fearless. Olivia liked that. In fact, when he worked, she couldn't take her eyes off of him. Just watching him made her hot. One of her fellow thespians informed her of Victor's amorous feelings towards her. It was that bit of information that prompted her to request Victor as a scene partner. After a few rehearsals, Olivia confessed to her part in their sudden pairing. Victor was absolutely delighted.

Though they were both aware of their mutual attraction, neither of them wanted to rush the 'getting to know you' part of their friendship. They had spent several evenings hanging out in every corner of the Windy City, running lines from the script wherever they went. Ironically, one of their favorite places to hang out happened to be right there on Clark Street in Wrigleyville. A place called Bar Louie. They spent a few consecutive nights there recently, deciding finally that they needed a quieter locale in which to work. Olivia invited him to her apartment on Argyle. Victor accepted her invitation. For the first time, they would be truly alone.

Olivia crossed her legs and gestured to Victor to sit down beside her. Victor scooped up the play and thumped clumsily onto the couch. "So where were we?" he asked.

"Well," Olivia began as she opened her copy of the Weller play. "We just finished with the section concerning the conditions of Paul and Susan's reunion."

"Right. If Paul wants her back, he has to move to New York. He'd rather stay in Boston."

"Yes, but don't forget," Olivia said while pointing an accusatory finger at Victor, "he wants to have children and she's not ready." She directed her attention back to the book and began scanning the text. She turned a page and pointed at the words at the top. "Oh. Here we are, at the top of page fifty-six. We were discussing the kiss."

A light tint of red filled Victor's cheeks. In their previous rehearsals, this particular part of the scene was always done with the dialogue only. Now, it was time to incorporate the blocking and the physical life of the scene. Victor had waited for this moment. He couldn't wait to press his lips against hers, to take in her scent and taste her for the first time. "Yeah. That's right."

"How should we play it?" Olivia asked. She pretended to be completely unaffected by the prospect of kissing Victor. She wanted to display professionalism and maturity. After all, this wasn't the first time she had to kiss someone during a scene for class. She had done many scenes that required a kiss, so why should this be any different? Olivia smiled, more to herself than Victor. This *was* different. For the first time, she wanted to kiss her scene partner without a script being the cause. This time, she wanted to throw herself on this man and toss the play out the window. "Should it be a quick peck on the cheek, or maybe on the lips? I mean, after all, they are still deciding whether or not to get back together."

"True," Victor agreed. "But," he paused. "They do miss each other and I think the kiss, their first in three months, should be indicative of that."

"Maybe so," Olivia said, tilting her head to the side as she considered Victor's suggestion. "But, after three months of being apart, they might be a little hesitant." Olivia fell silent. As badly as she wanted to kiss Victor, she didn't want to compromise a great scene by delivering the wrong kiss. She moved her gaze to Victor. He stared back at her. "Maybe we should test it out, you know, to see what feels right."

Victor froze. He knew what would feel right and he was positive it wasn't what the playwright had in mind when he wrote the scene. Still, he wanted the scene to be the best it could be so he buried his own desires and embodied the desires of his character. "Okay," he said. "Sounds good."

Olivia placed her copy of the play on the coffee table. She moved her face within inches of his. Their eyes met. The awkwardness from the unfamiliar closeness caused Olivia to smile uncontrollably. Victor felt it, too, and began to chuckle. Olivia slapped him playfully on his chest.

"Stop laughing," she said, attempting to stifle a giggle of her own.

"I'm trying," he said, laughing more nervously now.

Olivia moved in a little closer. "This won't work if we can't keep a straight face," she said. "We've got to get this right."

"We can try again later," Victor suggested, moving away slightly.

"No," Olivia said as she thrust herself back at him. At last, she had Victor where she'd wanted him for so long, she wasn't going to let a little discomfort stop her now. Her laughter fell away as she caressed the right side of his face with her left hand. "No," she repeated before pressing her lips firmly against his. Both of them released a heavy sigh as they relented and began to wrap their arms around each other. Within seconds, all thought or memory of the play had escaped them. This was not a kiss for the sake of their characters, this was a kiss steeped in their mutual passion.

Their heads turned from side to side as the kiss became more intense. Olivia released a small moan and pulled Victor even closer to her. She pushed her tongue into his mouth and began to run her hands through his hair. Victor followed suit and tightened his grip on her shapely frame. He moved his hands down her back and up again to the nape of her neck. Before long, Olivia's hands began probing under Victor's T-shirt and found quickly an avenue to the warm flesh within. She rubbed his tight stomach and was turned on even more as she felt each indentation of his abdominal muscles. "Mmm," she managed to utter through the intense kisses.

Victor maneuvered his hands around to the front of Olivia's blouse. He moved his hands cautiously in the direction of her large, firm breasts. Though Olivia had her hands under his T-shirt, he didn't want to disrespect her by assuming he could touch her most private parts. As if Olivia read his thoughts, she grabbed one of his hands with her own and moved it to her breasts. She squeezed his hand gently, giving him the go-ahead to enjoy himself without apprehension. It wasn't long before she realized that being rubbed through her blouse was only going to offer her so much pleasure. Without breaking contact with Victor's lips, she began unbuttoning her blouse, revealing slowly a black lace bra strapped tightly around her voluptuous assets.

Victor wasted no time moving within the boundaries of her open top. He wrapped his hands as best he could around her breasts and began massaging the hot, sweaty flesh beneath the lacy material. He kissed her neck, which caused her to release another heavy sigh. His hungry mouth found its way to the top her breasts. Olivia arched her back and thrust her chest towards him again. Her breathing became more audible as the heat and intensity rose. Slowly, he moved his mouth to the edge of the fabric, and with the fingers of his right hand, he pulled the delicate material aside. His tongue grazed her nipple, causing it to rise and harden. Olivia pulled his head closer and Victor sucked the entire nipple into his mouth.

The passion was becoming too much for Olivia to contain. She reached behind her back and unclasped her bra, causing it to fall to her waist. Her breasts sprang free in front of Victor, sending a hot rush of blood into his throbbing penis. He pulled Olivia closer to him. She lifted herself up and straddled him. She pushed Victor against the back of the sofa and began grinding her pubic bone into him. Victor placed one hand on each of her large, brown breasts and returned to the pleasurable task of kissing and sucking her nipples. He moved back and forth between the two breasts, making certain to take time to nestle his head between her cleavage. He didn't want to neglect a single inch of her.

Olivia slid her hips back slightly as she ran her left hand down Victor's body toward his groin. She reached her destination and moved her hand across the fabric of his pants, rubbing his hard, pulsing cock.

Victor began to plant kisses all over her upper torso. He moved his hands around her body and rubbed his way past the arch in the small of her back. He continued to probe lower until his hands were holding her round ass firmly in place against him.

Olivia began fumbling with Victor's belt buckle. With every passing second, she became hotter and hotter, only to become clumsier in regards to undoing the restraints that kept her from releasing his thick member. Victor brought one of his hands to his buckle to aid her. Olivia pulled the belt from the loop; Victor yanked the metal stem from its hole in the leather allowing Olivia to pull the belt open. She unfastened the top of his slacks with no problem and, dexterously, made short work of the zipper. She forced her way within the confines of his Banana Republic boxers and closed her hand around the hot rod of flesh that throbbed happily in response to her caressing touch. She gripped his cock and began to stroke it gently in rhythm with their breathing. Victor moaned his approval and began kissing his way back up her neck. His tongue left a warm trail of wetness as his mouth caressed her lips once more and they fell into a deep, passionate kiss. Their breathing intensified. Olivia massaged his cock in rhythm with the gyrations of their bodies. Before reaching the point of no return, Olivia, without warning, released Victor and jumped off the couch. Her knees were weak from the heat and the passion and she sank to the floor in front of him. "Wait," she said. She tried to catch her breath as she shook her head from side to side. "No. We can't do this now."

Victor, sitting there with his penis flailing aimlessly against his stomach, was caught completely off guard. "Why not? What's wrong?"

"This," Olivia responded. "Don't get me wrong, this is exactly what I want, but," She paused.

Victor began to nod as some of the blood began to return to his brain. "Oh. Right. This is supposed to be about our scene work."

"Well, yes, but no," she responded. "That's not what I meant."

Victor stared at her, confused. He was trying to make sense of what she was saying but found it difficult to focus. On the one hand, he was sitting on her couch with his fly open and his cock ready to go. On the other hand, Olivia sat on the floor in front of him with her blouse hanging open, revealing her full, gorgeous breasts. Despite the momentary disorientation and disappointment, Victor smiled at her. He couldn't believe how beautiful she was.

Olivia continued. "What I meant was...we had made a decision not to rush our friendship and let things happen naturally between us."

Victor chuckled. "It felt pretty natural to me."

She smiled. "You know what I mean. I don't want to jump into something hot and heavy with you and then look at you six months from now and wonder who the hell you are. I want to know you first. I really do."

Victor exhaled heavily. "That's probably the nicest compliment anyone has ever paid me."

Olivia giggled. "I try."

"You're right," Victor conceded. "Maybe we're going a little too fast."

"Maybe?" Olivia asked.

"Well, yeah," he answered. "We've been attracted to each other for quite some time and though I want to continue to get to know you, who says this isn't happening exactly as it should?"

Olivia had to think for a moment. "I don't know. I guess I just want this to be different."

Victor leaned forward. "Olivia. We communicate well, we share a passion for acting and we genuinely want to be real friends to each other. I'll admit we're just starting out but I think we have something here. Maybe you're right. Maybe we are rushing it, but maybe we're not.

I promise you, either way, I still want to know you for who you are. The good, the bad and the beautiful."

She smiled warmly. "Part of me feels the way you do, I just...I don't know, you know?"

"Hey," Victor said. "Whatever you want to do is fine by me. Although, that was pretty great."

Olivia raised a devilish eyebrow. "Hell yeah, it was." They laughed together for a moment. Suddenly, Olivia stopped and looked at Victor. There was an unusual gleam in her eyes.

"What?" Victor questioned. He could almost hear the wheels of her brain turning inside her head.

"Fate," she said.

"Excuse me."

"We'll let fate decide," she said as she stood. Her bra fell to the floor as she buttoned up her blouse halfway. She turned and began moving towards the small hallway. She called over her shoulder to him. "Follow me."

Victor stood. He pushed his hard penis back into their cotton dungeon and fastened his pants. He followed Olivia into the hallway and made a right turn at the end into her bedroom.

The room was almost as Victor had expected. The walls were white. There was a queen-sized bed placed against the center of the far wall. It was covered with a thick white comforter that was pulled back at the head to reveal lavender sheets underneath. There were several pictures on the wall, photos of family and friends that revealed small glimpses of Olivia's life. The sliding closet door was open half way and Victor took in the colorful blouses and slacks that hung from hangers over the wide array of shoes that sat well arranged on the floor below. A small night table stood by the bed. Olivia positioned herself by the table and directed Victor's gaze to a large book that rested on top. The title of the book was *"Fairy Tales for Today."* Olivia opened the cover of the book. There, sitting just beneath the hard cover, was a quarter. Olivia retrieved the coin and turned to Victor with a smile.

"This is my lucky quarter," she said. "Whenever I can't make an important decision where either consequence isn't too dire, I let fate decide."

Victor couldn't contain his grin. "We're going to flip a quarter?"

She laughed. "Yeah. Heads, we throw caution to the wind and go for it right here and now." She made a small head gesture towards the bed. "Tails, we abstain and see what happens down the road, taking into consideration that nothing may ever happen between us again. Either way, we promise to deal with the consequences of each as friends."

"You've really got this all thought out, don't you?" he asked.

"No, I don't. But my father always taught me that some things in life you just have to toss into the wind and say 'fuck it'. Let fate decide."

"You father taught you that, huh?"

"You bet. He's a great man." She held the quarter up. "So what do you say?"

Victor shrugged. One thing he knew for sure. He liked Olivia Tyler truly and no matter the outcome, it was a win-win situation. "Why not?"

"Great," she said. "It's *my* lucky quarter but this involves both of us." She thrust the quarter into his hand. "You flip."

Victor looked at the coin as if the weight of the world now rested on his shoulders. "You sure about this?"

"Again, no. But, my lucky quarter hasn't let me down yet."

Victor nodded. "Okay." He grabbed the quarter and balanced it atop the thumb of his left hand.

Olivia took a sudden step forward. "Wait," she demanded. She reached out and caressed Victor's face. She brought her lips to his and pressed firmly. She breathed heavily into his mouth. Finally, after several seconds, she pulled away and looked into his eyes. "Just in case it never happens again."

Victor smiled. He hoped that it would happen again. If not, he knew that he'd found someone special.

Without uttering a sound, Olivia stood back anxiously and nodded to Victor.

He looked at her and said, "You're beautiful. Thank you."

She winked.

They both fell silent as they eyed the quarter that balanced on Victor's thumb. Victor took a deep breath, exhaled slowly, and then flipped the quarter into the air.

The End

Printed in the United States
43437LVS00004B/43